Criminal Intent

Patsy Collins

The author can be found at
www.patsycollins.uk

ISBN: 978-1914339-10-3

To all those who've ever made me feel murderous – this is my revenge!

Contents

1. Murder In Mind

Becky was glad to see Annette on the bus that rainy morning. She wanted to moan about her husband – better that than brood until she got annoyed out of all proportion.

"Remember Dale bought whole tinned tomatoes, as they were a penny cheaper than chopped?" Becky said, trying not to drip on her friend.

"Didn't you convince him it wasn't worth the hassle?"

"Yeah. After I made him do the chopping."

"So, what's the problem?" Annette asked.

"He wants lasagna again, but won't pay for fresh basil. Admittedly that does cost a bit, but it's not the same without."

"Pick yew leaves from the churchyard for his portion!"

"I thought they were poisonous?" Becky asked.

"Exactly. They'll halve your food bills!"

Becky grinned. Annette always cheered her up by letting her moan about Dale's annoying little traits and thinking up creative ways to get revenge. She'd suggested blocking out the sound of snoring with a thick pillow held over Dale's nose until he was quiet. The over the top solutions made Becky giggle and helped her get things into perspective.

Becky tried to do the same for Annette. Her Ross seemed a pain.

"He cancelled a golf match because I said I didn't want to go," Annette said once. "I'd just fancied reading my book in peace, but couldn't tell him without hurting his feelings."

"Say you've taken up gardening, then read in the shed."

"He'd just come out every five minutes to check I was OK, ask if I wanted a cup of tea, or if he should start making dinner."

Annette often said he was kind and thoughtful, but Becky worried what those thoughts were. Once Annette mentioned a new coffee shop she'd heard served wonderful cakes and that she hoped to visit as soon as Ross could take her.

"How about we go together on Saturday?" Becky said.

"Sorry, but we're out for the day."

Becky had made several similar suggestions since the two woman had met on the bus journey to work. Annette always replied Ross had made plans, or she'd have to check with Ross, making it clear she couldn't consider going anywhere without him. The only exception was work, and even then he walked her to the bus stop and met her again afterwards.

"He works from home," Annette explained once. "He says walking with me gets him in the mood to work and meeting me later helps him switch off from it."

That was plausible, but Becky thought he might also be checking up on her.

Belatedly Becky noticed Annette was completely dry, despite the rain and lack of umbrella. "Wasn't it raining where you live?"

"Ross carried the brolly and needed it to go back home," she'd said.

Had he made sure she didn't have one with her, so it would be less likely she'd go anywhere in her lunch break? "How is he anyway?" Becky asked.

"He's fine. Yesterday he surprised me by taking me out to

lunch, wasn't that sweet of him?"

"Lovely," Becky said, wondering what would happen if Annette had decided to go shopping or anything else without clearing it with him first.

Or maybe she was just jealous as Dale never surprised her in a way which cost him money. Even her engagement ring had been a family heirloom. Not that she'd minded – it was gorgeous and she was touched that his family wanted her to have it, especially as hers lived so far away.

Dale had always been careful with money. When they met he'd been saving to start his own car repair business and for the first few years of their marriage every penny went into paying back the loan he'd taken out. He'd not got into the habit of spending much since, but neither had he been mean until they got a smart meter. She hadn't minded when he suggested they turn the heating down in the evenings. They usually just watched TV, which they could do just as well snuggled up together under a blanket. Actually she was sleeping better now the bedroom was cooler at nights.

Measuring the right amount of water to boil in the kettle, although a bit of a faff, was sensible too, but once he realised such simple actions saved money, he became obsessive. He wouldn't turn on a light unless he considered it absolutely necessary.

"Put Lego bricks at the top of the stairs to prove it's a good idea to put the light on if either of you get up in the night," Annette had suggested when Becky told her.

Dale hunted for bargains in the supermarket and watered down washing-up liquid and other cleaners to 'make them go further'.

"Do you do the same thing with customers' brake fluid?" Becky had demanded.

"Of course not! That would be dangerous and I'm responsible for the safety of my customers."

His own safety would be at risk if she ever got totally fed up enough to out one of Annette's schemes. Thank goodness she could let off steam joking about them.

"You look serious," Annette said.

"I was just thinking about where to get yew leaves."

"You don't want to do it," Annette said. "Too obvious. It'd be better if I did and you sorted out Ross."

"Oh?"

"He gets on my nerves," Annette confessed. "He's kind and thoughtful, but I feel completely smothered."

"I didn't like to say, but I was getting that impression."

"That's a plan then? We'll bump them off and afterwards we'll meet for coffee whenever we like. I'll be allowed out alone, and you'll be able to 'waste' money on a little treat."

Becky laughed uncomfortably.

"We'll have to plan it carefully, so we've both got good alibis of course."

Annette seemed to have put some thought into it, and Becky recalled that all her revenge schemes showed she had murder in mind.

Becky didn't want to kill anyone, or have her husband killed. It wasn't just that she was squeamish about murder – she really wanted Dale to stay alive. She loved him and knew they just needed to communicate better.

That night Becky told Dale exactly what she thought about his penny pinching.

"I'm sorry, love. I thought you'd got so used to saving money you wouldn't notice what I was up to."

"What are you talking about?"

"I've been saving to take you to Australia to visit your sister and nieces."

"Oh, Dale, really?"

"Yes, really. I even phoned your boss to make sure you'd be able to have the time off."

"Good job I didn't have you killed then!"

"What are you talking about?" Dale echoed her words of a few moments previously.

Becky told him about her conversations with Annette.

"You never really meant any of it, did you?"

"Of course not. And I don't think she did either... but what if she did? She's been suppressing her annoyance a long time. It's possible she might do something drastic."

"Maybe we should tell the police? Just in case."

"Let's go into the station. I'll explain better in person."

On the way they passed the new coffee shop. Becky, remembering Annette's plan to visit when she had no husband to stop her going out, glanced in the window. No, it couldn't be ...

"Stop the car!"

"What is it?"

"I just saw Annette. She was with a man and tipping something into his drink!"

Dale braked sharply.

Becky leapt out and ran into the shop. "Don't drink it, Ross!" she yelled.

Both Annette and Ross stared at her open mouthed, then burst out laughing. "I was just telling Ross I thought I'd worried you with my silly joke."

Becky noticed the empty sugar sachet in Annette's hand and laughed herself from relief.

Dale arrived and asked, "Everything OK?"

"Yes. Well, Annette isn't trying to kill Ross. I'm not sure if she's going to forgive me for accusing her of it though."

"Of course I do. Sit down and join us both of you."

"Might as well," Dale said. "I've put a pound in the meter and don't want to waste the money." He winked at Becky to show he was teasing, then proved it by ordering them both hot chocolates with whipped cream.

"What I can't understand is why anyone would think Annette wanted me dead," Ross said.

"It's because you fuss over me too much. After the accident I did need a lot of help, and I really appreciate everything you've done for me. But I don't need constant care now and feel totally smothered." She spoke sharply and Ross looked rather shocked.

Becky, thinking it would be better if they discussed it alone after having time to think, moved the conversation along. "Sorry about your accident, Annette. Sounds as though it was awful."

"It was," Ross confirmed. "The worst thing is that although we and the police know who did it, he wasn't taken to court because of some technicality. He's still drinking and driving."

"He's bound to crash again," said Dale. "I sort out so many cars damaged that way."

"He could kill someone next time," said Ross.

The men exchanged glances.

"Or die himself in a horrible accident?" Dale suggested.

2. I Don't Like Cheats

Penny Alderman is annoying in so many ways. She thinks she's better than me, that's the real trouble. No, tell a lie, the REAL problem is she often seems to be proved right.

Her grades at school were always that bit better than mine. Her hair was shinier. She married sooner than me to someone much better off. Someone who didn't leave her to deal with a crippling mortgage and pitying looks.

She isn't better though. She cheats. She did it at school – copied coursework contributed to her good grades. She got pregnant on purpose, to trap that husband of hers. And later she cheated on him.

The final straw was the cake competition. For years she's won that. I didn't know until recently as I don't usually attend the village show. It's always on the bank holiday, and I'm needed in the Rose and Ferret on bank holidays, and weekends, and all the other times the likes of Penny want someone to cook for them instead of lifting a finger herself.

It's not just Sunday roasts and evening dinners I do, but cakes and the like. Eat in or take away. It was one of mine which won Penny the prize, I'm sure of it. Iced it up fancy she had, so I wouldn't have known except for the look on her face. I've seen that expression before.

There didn't seem much point in saying anything. Nobody would have believed me, would they? You can't prove who baked a particular cake, especially once it's been eaten – and she donated that one to the tea sales pretty sharpish. Then she said she wasn't going to enter in future. She'd give someone else a chance. Maybe she felt guilty, more likely she'd realised that with me in the know she couldn't get away with it again.

I don't like cheats, but my courses of action were limited.

You've probably heard the advice about writing letters you'll never send, to people who annoy you. The idea is you rant as much as you like, swear, threaten – whatever you fancy. Then once you've got everything off your chest, you'll feel better. Perhaps even decide you've over reacted. It doesn't work. Writing to Penny just reminded me of every single thing she'd done to annoy me.

Slightly more satisfying would have been to write the letter AND send it. That was tempting, but not realistic. Somehow I couldn't tell her all that to her face, and signing the thing and shoving it through her door was beyond me. That's why people like her keep getting away with stuff, isn't it? Nobody dares put them right.

The thought of not signing did cross my mind. Poison pen letters they're called, when you send them anonymously. But if I left out all the bits which would tell her it was me, there wouldn't be much virtual poison.

Real poison seemed a better bet. It's hard to get someone to eat a letter, unless they're a baby or a dog and I have nothing against either. There is one kind of paper people eat though – rice paper. That's the thin coating on the bottom of nougat and macaroons. We have a stock in the Rose and Ferret. I ordered quite a lot a while back, and make a batch of macaroons now and then, to justify doing so. I wrote on a sheet, then baked a cake, using a special extra ingredient. Penny will have to eat a slice, because once she stopped competing in the village competition she was asked to be judge. That means tasting the entries. I entered under a false name – a poison pen cake!

I know it'll work as I've done it before. My husband you see. When I said he left, I didn't mean it in the dearly departed way, not at first. His death came after I'd kicked him out. In fact right after he tasted the cake I sent him. The one with two letters. A faked note, on scented notepaper, rested on top of the box. 'Something sweet for my sweet' it said and was apparently signed by his mistress. Another, written on rice paper and signed by me was baked into the bottom. That one said, 'I know you cheated on me with Penny. I don't like cheats'.

The one I've written to Penny, and which I've baked into the bottom of my entry says much the same thing. Judging starts just about now, so she'll be dead within minutes.

You know, I'm feeling better already.

3. Murder At Solent Castle

"Remember the murder holes I showed you earlier?" George the tour guide asked.

Adam and the rest of his class did. They were above the castle entrance. Any soldiers waiting above could fire arrows or drop things onto anyone trying to force their way in.

"Look over there," George pointed to the corner of the big room.

Everyone went over to look down on the visitors who were queuing up at the ticket office which was in what had once been a guardroom, just past the portcullis.

"See how easy it would be to fire at them from here, or drop stuff on their heads?"

The class agreed it would.

The tour guide's radio made a noise. "Excuse me," he said and then spoke into it. "George here. Go ahead." He listened for a moment, then said, "Understood." He switched the radio off.

Adam thought this seemed odd as it had been turned on all the rest of the time. The class had heard messages about a group who'd be late, another coming early and an unexpectedly high number of private visitors. A couple of times people were asked to go to the manager's office or other places. Why would George only decide to turn it off now?

The guide smiled and then started talking as though nothing had happened. Maybe Miss Jenkins was right and Adam did imagine mysteries when there were none.

George said, "And see this lever here. If I released it, the portcullis would come crashing down. Then how would our enemies escape whatever the soldiers up here decided to do?"

Adam remembered learning about the narrow entrances and passageways which stopped lots of people coming in at once and the spiral stairs all turning the same way so defending soldiers could use their swords much more easily than the attackers could. Solent Castle also had a special trip step in most stairs, which were a different size from all the others and could catch out anyone who didn't know which one it was.

George had given a health and safety talk to lots of people, not just Adam's class. He explained that although the castle had recently undergone a lengthy restoration process and been made as safe as possible they hadn't managed to make the stone walls and floors soft. There was a horrible man in an orange coat who talked all the way through. He didn't even say nice things and Adam was certain he wasn't the only one who wanted to listen to George instead.

Even after they'd been warned about the low doorways and the trip step, a couple of people had banged their heads or stumbled. Adam could easily imagine how much worse it would be for anyone wearing a metal helmet and armour, and carrying a sword. The defences were all really clever, but it seemed as though they wouldn't always be put to the test if the enemy were attacked before they got in.

When Adam realised the rest of the class didn't have an

answer to George's question about the murder holes, he put up his hand. "They couldn't," he suggested. "They wouldn't be able to get in to attack, and they couldn't even run away if more soldiers were behind them."

"Exactly right. Obviously you've been paying attention."

Adam was pleased with the tour guide's praise, but a little disappointed to see Miss Jenkins was talking to someone else and hadn't noticed.

"Would they pour boiling oil down the murder holes?" a classmate asked.

"If they'd had time to heat it up they might, but there are lots of other things they could use." The guide told them about people emptying pots which had been used for toilets on the attackers.

"Class, can I have your attention please?" Miss Jenkins looked worried.

Why? She must know by now that they liked all the gruesome details best.

"We have to go now," she said.

"Oooh, Miss he was just getting to the best bit!"

"It's not fair, Miss. There's loads we haven't seen."

The lady Miss Jenkins had been talking to said something to the tour guide, who nodded at her.

"Right kids, I want you in your pairs like your teacher had you earlier on," George said. "You're going to follow me outside, nice and quietly, and we'll go and take a look at the moat."

A few people complained, but the guide was heading for the stairs. He asked Miss Jenkins and the other lady to go last, which Adam guessed was to make sure nobody got left behind. He couldn't work out why they were going outside now though. The guide had promised to take them right up to the top of the biggest tower so they could look down and see all the defences. That would include the moat. It didn't make sense that they'd go outside again first. There must be a fire or something and George didn't want anyone to panic.

As they made their way outside they saw other groups of people were also being directed back to the car park area and that the entrance was closed. Once outside Adam saw a police car, but no policemen so he didn't know if his friend and hero PC Marks was involved. The police officers must already be inside. Surely they wouldn't be if there was a fire? You should never go into a burning building, and there wasn't any smoke.

The guide led them to the moat. When they got there Miss Jenkins decided they should have their lunch early. They hardly heard her over the sound of sirens. An ambulance and another police car arrived, but no fire engine. Something was definitely going on! In the hope of finding out what it was, Adam volunteered to go with George to get everyone's lunch bags from the minibus. He was rewarded. The guide switched his radio back on to report that Adam's group were all safely outside and about to have lunch.

"Good. If you can leave them, come back to the staffroom. The police suspect it's murder, so obviously they'll need to speak to everyone."

"Murder!" Adam gasped.

"You shouldn't have heard that," the guide said, but not until after he'd said a word Adam guessed was something else he wasn't supposed to have heard.

It didn't make much difference, as by the time they'd collected the lunches and taken them back to where Miss

Jenkins was waiting with the rest of the class, lots of people were talking about a body. The word murder was said several times.

Murder was the most serious crime ever and Adam was right there when it happened! This was even more exciting than hearing all the gruesome stuff about medieval battles. He must think really carefully; perhaps he'd seen a clue. Maybe even spotted the victim or the killer.

The horrible lying man! It could be him.

"Miss, there's been a murder," he told Miss Jenkins.

"Adam, I doubt that… " She stopped talking and stared at the tour guide. "Oh. Oh dear."

"Miss, I have to talk to the police. I might be able to help."

Miss Jenkins moved a little way off and beckoned Adam to follow. She spoke quietly. "I know how much you want to be a policeman and you are very clever, but this won't be something your friend PC Marks will be involved with, and it isn't something you can help with."

"But, Miss, I might have seen who did it."

"That is possible, we've seen a lot of people."

"I don't mean like that. There was one man who looked a bit like Donald Trump and he was wearing a great big orange coat and he's a liar!"

"Did you see him do anything strange?"

"I don't know," Adam admitted. "I just noticed that he was a liar, but I don't know how I knew." Even to him it didn't sound very convincing.

"Sadly people lie all the time," Miss Jenkins said.

That was true – and it didn't mean they were criminals.

PC Marks had told him that. Sometimes people didn't want to come forward as witnesses as they'd been doing something they shouldn't have but which had nothing to do with the crime being investigated. Even so, Adam thought he should tell someone about his suspicions.

He didn't have long to wait, as PC Marks came into school later that week. He told everyone, not just Adam's class, that murder and other violent crimes were actually very rare. After that he told them lots of stuff about how they could stay safe. Adam listened politely, even though his friend had already told him. He listened far more intently to all the details of what would be done to catch whoever had committed the horrible crime at Solent Castle and how they would be sent to prison for a very long time, so they couldn't do it again.

It was almost lunchtime when he'd finished talking and the headteacher said they could all go for their break early and that PC Marks would stay to talk to anyone who was worried or had questions. Adam waited until the policeman was on his own.

"You OK, deputy?" his friend asked.

"Yes. We didn't see anything horrible and it was sort of exciting to be there when it happened and see the police cars arriving."

"Miss Jenkins tells me you thought you saw something."

"I didn't see anyone get shot or anything, but there was a man there who was a liar. Miss thinks I made it up because I want to be involved with the investigation. I didn't, honest."

"I know you wouldn't do that. So, what happened?"

"I can't remember exactly why I knew, but just as we

were going into the castle there was a man telling lies, like he wanted everyone to hear him."

"One of the staff?"

"No, a visitor. He looked like President Trump and he had a huge coat which came down nearly to his knees. He wasn't orange, but the coat was."

"He should be easy to spot on the CCTV then."

"Can I help you look?"

"Sorry, deputy. I'm not a detective so I'm not actively involved in the investigation. Although it happened at the castle it's not thought to be a local crime, so I…"

"That's it! I remember now why I thought the man was lying. He said a lot about not having been to the area before and it wasn't true."

"How do you know?"

"I… I don't know, sorry. I can't believe it; I was actually on the scene and I'm no help. Maybe Miss Jenkins is right and I'm just imagining someone is a suspect because I want to feel involved."

"Don't worry, lad. It would have been surprising if you did see anything and you were right to tell me about your suspicions. There's no telling what little detail could be useful."

Adam felt better after talking to his friend. He felt even better the next day when Mum and Dad said PC Marks had arranged to take him to talk to some of the people who were investigating the murder. They had heard of his interest in becoming a policeman and that he'd helped solve crimes and had offered to show him some of their techniques for gathering evidence. "That's if you'd like to go?"

If Mum couldn't work that out there was no chance of her

becoming a detective!

After school on Friday, Adam was introduced to two scenes of crime investigators. One was introduced as Detective Constable Tim and the other was Detective Sergeant Suzy.

"I expect you know that we collect fingerprints?" Detective Tim asked.

"Yes. PC Marks showed me how to do that and took mine once and then I did my brother and Mum and Dad's."

"Ah, that's from the suspects, but we also need to collect them at the crime scene." He showed Adam how a special light could be used to look for fingerprints. Once they were found they could then be treated with chemicals or powder so they showed up better and were then photographed or collected on sticky tape.

Detective Tim gave Adam a plate. "There was a doughnut on here. Can you find the fingerprint and prove who took it?"

Using the light, Adam soon spotted the fingerprint and then dusted it with powder.

"Right, now you need to find out who left it there. How will you do that?"

"Look at the suspect's fingerprints?" Adam said.

"It went missing just after you arrived, so who are your suspects?"

Adam didn't like to say it, but the answer seemed obvious. "You and Sergeant Suzy."

"You and PC Marks don't eat doughnuts then?"

Oh dear. It was probably well known locally that the pair of them often did share the flask of tea and the bag of doughnuts that Mum gave him when he was allowed to go on the beat with PC Marks. Surely detective Tim didn't really think either of them had stolen his doughnut?

"Looking at the position of the print, I'd say it was likely to be a thumb print," PC Marks said.

Adam thought he could be right. "It's quite big. Bigger than mine." He put his own thumb close to the print, but didn't touch it.

"OK, that's you out then," Detective Tim said.

Adam looked carefully at PC Marks' thumbs. The patterns were quite different. Sergeant Suzy's looked too small as well as being much more swirly than the one on the plate. Detective Tim's was a perfect match!

"It was you!" Adam said. "You took the doughnut."

"OK, I admit it. Luckily I bought them, so it's not a crime. Even more luckily that means it's Sergeant Suzy's turn to buy the next lot. How about we stop off on the way to the crime scene?"

"Yes please," Adam said. Wow, he was going with actual detectives to an actual crime scene. Maybe he'd find a clue!

"Where's the best bakery around here?" Sergeant Suzy asked. "Is there one in South Wick?"

"I don't know where that is," Adam said.

"I think she means Southwick," PC Marks said. "The w is silent," he explained to the detectives. "Trips up a lot of non-locals, that does."

"Oh!" Adam said. He'd just remembered that his orange coated suspect hadn't made that mistake.

"What is it?" Sergeant Suzy asked.

Adam explained. "But it doesn't prove anything. He said they were staying in a B&B there, so someone probably told him the right way to say it."

They stopped to buy doughnuts in the bakery in Little Mallow and ate them on the way.

Solent Castle was open to visitors again. Adam loved it when the police officers all showed their badges at the ticket office and explained that Adam was with them, so he didn't have to buy a ticket!

As they all made their way to the crime scene, Detective Tim stumbled on a trip step in the spiral stairway. "Blood... um, blast, I forgot about that."

"Oh!" Adam said again as another memory came back. The man in the orange coat hadn't tripped, but his companion did. That's it – he was a bit mean saying how clumsy she was. Adam remembered he'd been talking to her instead of listening properly to the safety briefing, yet he'd been ahead of her and hadn't stumbled himself.

He explained this to the three police officers. "She might have hurt herself and people don't like to be called clumsy, especially if they are. He wasn't very nice at all, but earlier he'd been telling people they'd just got married and how happy they were. I think he was lying about that and when he said he'd never been here before. He wouldn't have known about the trip step unless he had."

Detective Tim and Sergeant Suzy looked at each other, then they asked PC Marks if any details about the victim were common knowledge.

"I don't believe so," he said. "Adam, have you heard anything about the type of person who was murdered?"

"Not really. Some people have guessed who they think it is, but I don't think they know. Oh! Did I get it wrong and it was Mr Orange Coat who was shot?"

"Will you describe him again for me, please?"

Adam did his best to give as many details as he could, including the information that he was about as tall as Detective Tim, but a lot fatter. "He wasn't fat like a lady going to have a baby, it was all over. Even his face and his hands were quite fat."

"No, he wasn't the victim," sergeant Suzy said. "And nobody was shot." Then she asked if the lying man had been wearing gloves.

"No. So if he was the murderer there might be fingerprints?"

"We did find some which don't match any members of staff."

"They might be from other visitors," Adam suggested.

"Unlikely in the place where the victim was found. Come on, we'll show you. On the way perhaps you could describe the person with your man in the orange coat?"

Adam told them all he could remember about the lady. It was harder to say what she'd looked like as she hadn't reminded him of anyone, but he did remember her lime green coat. "They looked like orange and lime tic tac sweets," he said.

"Did you see either of them again?" Sergeant Suzy asked.

"I don't know. I thought I saw him when we were having lunch, but it might just have been someone in the same colour coat. I only saw his back and probably thought it was him because he was with another lady in a lime green coat."

"Not the same one?"

"It wasn't the same lady. Maybe she was her friend and borrowed the coat? That did look exactly the same."

"Can you describe this other lady?"

Adam did his best. "Sorry, that's a bit rubbish. I've made her sound the same, but she wasn't. The first one seemed like she didn't want to be noticed, not like the man and the second lady."

"You're a very good witness, Adam. Thank you."

He wasn't sure which was the best, praise from a detective sergeant or being allowed to duck under the tape which said 'Police crime scene do not cross'. Once they were all under that, Detective Tim unlocked a door and led them into a secret passage. That would have been really good even if it wasn't a crime scene.

"This area isn't open to the public because it's so narrow and there's only one way in and out," Detective Tim explained. "Staff don't come in very often either, but we were lucky and one of the guides had decided to bring his girlfriend here to... well, they found the body and immediately alerted the authorities."

The detectives showed Adam and PC Marks where the body had been found and the location of the fingerprints.

"Oh no, I touched that beam," Adam said.

"It's OK, we've collected all the evidence we need from here already. You are right to be concerned though. It's very important that no one touches or moves anything at a crime scene. Remember that when you're a policeman and you'll be doing a lot to help catch criminals."

After Adam had finished looking round, Sergeant Suzy asked Adam if he would make a statement about the things he'd told them.

"A real proper one which will be evidence?"

"Yes. We might want you to talk to someone who'll try to make a picture of the people you saw too."

"Wow!"

PC Marks said, "He means yes, he's willing to make a statement."

"Can we leave you to talk to his parents and bring him in?" Sergeant Suzy asked.

"My pleasure."

The next day, Mum came with him to the police station. Detective Suzy shook her hand and thanked them both for coming.

"No problem," Mum said. "Adam is eager to help and PC Marks has explained what you want and why."

First they looked at CCTV footage. It was in black and white and jumped about like it was on fast forward, even though it wasn't. Even so, Adam pointed out the man and lady he had seen, and then they saw his class and Miss Jenkins arrive. The tour guide who took the class round talked to everyone first, telling them about minding their heads and being careful not to fall and all that. You couldn't hear anything on the tape, but Adam remembered enough to explain what was happening. They could all see the man was talking to people the whole time.

The people who were going round on their own went away and George the tour guide talked just to Adam's class.

"He was telling us about how people might try to get into the castle in the history days," Adam explained.

As they watched, they saw the orange coated man walking up the spiral stairs and the lady follow him and stumble on the trip step.

Adam was really pleased that it showed all the things he said had happened.

Next Adam was taken to see a man who asked lots of

questions about what the man and ladies Adam had seen looked like. He made pictures of them on his computer. He showed Adam how he'd done it and explained that he'd use images from the CCTV too, to help get them accurate.

Mum sat with him while he gave his statement. Sergeant Suzy asked him lots of questions and made notes. Then she read back what he said each time and asked him if it was correct. She got everything exactly right. Adam couldn't answer every question, but Sergeant Suzy said that didn't matter; the things he did know were very useful.

"Thank you, Adam. If you do happen to think of anything else, or realise you've made a mistake, then please let us know."

She gave Mum a card with her telephone number on it and another one to ring up if she or Adam were at all worried or upset.

"Adam, PC Marks has told me how helpful you've been to him in other cases. I really do hope you will become a police officer one day as you will be an asset to the service."

"Thank you."

"Do you know what the word confidential means?"

"Like a secret."

"Exactly. What I'm going to tell you now will soon be public knowledge, but until you see it on the news or in the paper I must ask you to keep it confidential."

"I promise and Mum won't tell anyone, will you?"

She agreed that she wouldn't.

"The lady who tripped was the victim."

"Oh!"

"I know it can't be very nice to know you saw her so soon

beforehand. I hope it helps to know that what you've told us will help us catch the person who did this and stop him doing it to anyone else."

"So, is he… " Mum said. "The man Adam saw is the one…?"

"He is our main suspect now, yes. As you've just heard, he claimed they were both newlyweds. If that's true, it's rather odd that he hasn't reported her missing, don't you think?"

Adam and Mum both agreed it was suspicious.

The next day on the news Adam heard the victim described and saw the pictures that he'd help make, so he was able to tell his friends all about going to give a statement. They all watched the news every night after that to see if the killer had been caught. It was a long time before he was.

Adam knew before all his friends, because one day PC Marks arrived with a bag of doughnuts. "These are a present for you, from Sergeant Suzy. She also asked me to give you this." PC Marks handed him an envelope. On it was written 'Confidential. For the attention of Adam'.

The letter inside explained that the man in the orange coat had been arrested. It said that as other people, including George the tour guide, had seen what happened during the health and safety briefing and this was captured on CCTV then Adam wouldn't be required to give evidence in court. That didn't mean that he hadn't helped them a lot because he had.

The police had discovered the man in the orange suit was telling the truth about just having got married and the first lady in the lime green coat was both his wife and the victim. He hadn't told the truth about never having been to the castle before. He'd been one of the people who'd restored Solent Castle, so would have known about the trip step and the secret passage.

Sergeant Suzy believed he'd kept a key at the time and had been planning the murder even then. Not long after he'd returned to his home town, he had married a lady who had a lot of money. They'd moved away after the wedding, so his new neighbours hadn't realised that the lady he came back from honeymoon with wasn't really his wife. It was believed that lady had gone alone to Solent Castle and after Mr Orange Coat killed his new wife, she had put on the dead woman's coat and pretended to be her ever since.

The letter ended by saying that this had to be proved in court, so until after the trial Adam had to keep the information confidential and tell no one but his parents and PC Marks.

"Come on, deputy; what does it say? That's if you're allowed to tell me?"

Wow! Adam was the first to know! He was so happy that he could hardly speak, so he gave his friend the letter to read and went to get glasses of milk for them to drink with their doughnuts.

4. The Archaeologist's Dilemma

For years my boss, Professor Bishop, looked down my blouse, and his nose. "History and women don't mix," he'd sneered. "Your brains are a blunt tool."

He dug himself into a hole as I scraped away earth.

I learned something surprising.

The professor was torn between dismissing my findings and taking the credit.

After a few minutes of listening to him attempt to do both at once, I had my own dilemma. Should I prove his patronising statements wrong by revealing the celebrated medieval scholar we'd unearthed was actually female? Or would it be better to rebury that discovery along with my sharpened pickaxe which is now penetrating the professor's skull?

5. Cat Burglar

Granny and Grandad – Summer 1993

Grandad wondered if he'd done the right thing, agreeing to bring little Julian to the jumble sale. They'd been on their way to the park when Granny saw the sign.

"Let's look in for a few minutes," she'd said. Granny liked to buy woollen items and undo them and knit other things with them. Grandad liked to do whatever Granny wanted him to like doing.

Grandad had slipped Julian a toffee when they went in, which kept him quiet for a short time. The lad wasn't tall enough even to see what was on the tables so would soon be getting bored unless he, like Granny, had something to look out for.

Bending down, apparently to tie his laces, Grandad placed a coin right where Julian was about to walk.

Julian – Summer 1993

Six-year-old Julian spotted a penny on the ground.

"Look, Granny!" he said, tugging at her cardigan.

"Pick it up then. It will bring you good luck," she told him.

After that Julian was content to walk slowly round the

27

church hall, studying the floor for further treasure. He discovered a cardboard box. In it were some plastic bags, an empty drink can, two broken coat-hangers and a cat ornament.

Granny and Grandad already had one cat ornament, maybe they'd like that one to go with it? They often gave him presents and he wanted to give them something.

The lady running the stall didn't want to take his penny and said he could have the cat, so now he had two treasures! Jumble sales were fun.

Granny and Grandad – Christmas 1999

"I'm not sure I did the right thing," Granny said.

"I expect you did, love." Grandad wasn't sure what Granny was talking about, but that didn't mean he didn't know the correct response.

"It seemed so at the time, but now…" She was holding one of those ugly cat things little Julian had given them. "Maybe we shouldn't have been so enthusiastic over the first one."

"Perhaps not," Grandad, having noted the shift from I to we, agreed. "But it was thoughtful of him to think of giving us a gift and he's a sensitive lad. It seemed only right to encourage him."

"That's true, but if you hadn't acted quite so thrilled with the first cat he might not have bought another. That latest one is even more hideous than ever and it looks as though he's planning to give us one every Christmas and birthday forever more."

"You're right there." Grandad had no trouble looking

genuinely sorry.

Julian – Grandad's birthday 2003

Grandad had asked for a bar of chocolate for his birthday this year. "Your Granny will say it's not good for me, but she might let me eat it if it comes from you," he'd said.

At fifteen Julian was old enough to work out what was going on; Grandad knew Julian didn't have much pocket money, so had asked for something cheap. That was so nice of him that Julian was more determined than ever to get him something he'd really like.

The charity shop seemed a good place to try. Ever since discovering treasure at a jumble sale when he was little, he quite liked looking round places like that. His search was rewarded with the discovery of a cat ornament. It was only 25p, Julian could buy that for Grandad and still have enough money left to either buy a shiny box to put it in, or a small bar of chocolate.

The cat ornament fitted into the box perfectly, so buying that was obviously the right thing to do.

Granny and Grandad – 2004

"I'm worried about Julian," Granny said.

"Me too," Grandad said.

"He used to be such a nice boy and full of enthusiasm. Always showing us things he'd drawn or made. Kind too. Every Christmas and birthday he's bought us a little gift despite having no money."

"Those awful cats," Grandad said, with feeling.

"Well, yes but it's the thought which counts. You might have been a bit more enthusiastic about that last one. You know he can be sensitive, quick to be hurt."

"You're right, as usual," Grandad admitted. "That's why he failed his exams, I reckon. When that girlfriend of his lost interest in him, it knocked his confidence and he didn't try very hard."

"We need to do something about that."

"I'll talk to him," Grandad said. The look Granny gave him didn't do much for his own confidence, but Grandad wisely didn't mention it.

Julian – 2005

Julian's poor grandparents had been burgled. Granny had woken up in the night, saying she'd heard banging and that there was a draught. She claimed Grandad must have left a window open somewhere. He'd gone downstairs and surprised the thieves – and himself. Fortunately they'd fled without hurting him, but they hadn't left empty handed.

Julian had rushed round as soon as he heard the news. Grandad had been calmly giving the details to the insurance company, but Granny was distraught. She felt bad for putting Grandad in danger. "What would I do without him?" she'd said and, "Why did the old fool listen to me?"

Julian nearly replied cheekily with, 'Because you're always right' as that's what Grandad usually said to her, but he stopped himself. Grandad wasn't a fool and Julian didn't know what any of the family would do without him. He was always helping out and giving advice. After Julian's terrible exam results Grandad had taken Julian aside and said that he shouldn't worry so much about things.

"With some people it takes a while for their talents to develop and to understand what they want to do. These days, I just wait for your Granny to tell me, but before I met her I had to figure it out for myself and that's just what you're going to have to do."

Julian had stayed on at school and retaken his exams. The results had been better, but he still couldn't find a job he'd like and as far as Julian was aware he had no particular skills. He didn't have any money either, so couldn't buy Granny and Grandad a gift to cheer them up after the burglary. It was perhaps thinking about what they'd lost which drew his attention to a cat ornament in the window of the antique shop. He didn't need to read the tag to know he couldn't afford it.

Also in the antique dealer's shop window was a poster advertising a job vacancy. From television programmes Julian had watched with his grandparents, Julian understood that an antique dealer didn't just stand in a shop all day. They went to sales and auctions looking for interesting items, drove around the countryside, advised famous people and made important discoveries. It sounded interesting, but was it something he could do?

Julian thought about the burglary at Granny and Grandad's house. All the ornaments he'd bought them for Christmas and birthdays, from jumble sales and charity shops, even rescued from a skip in one case, had been taken. Lots of other things were left behind, including quite valuable cutlery they'd had as a wedding present and real crystal glasses received as anniversary gifts. Just cash, some bits of jewellery and bank cards, plus his gifts, were stolen.

The thieves must have recognised the cats as valuable. Julian hadn't. There was no point trying to convince anyone, even himself, that he'd actually known anything about the ornaments, but didn't it prove he had a good eye? Some kind of instinct?

Granny and Grandad – Just before lunch 2018

"It's all our doing you know," Granny said.

Grandad glanced around the edge of his newspaper. "It is?" He wasn't too nervous; she'd said our, not your.

"Young Julian's success, I mean. To think, a grandson of ours is on the television!"

"Ah. Yes," Grandad agreed enthusiastically. "Since he took that job at the antique shop he's doing really well. He's put so much effort and enthusiasm into it that he deserves his reward."

"And to think, if I hadn't encouraged him by being so nice about those terrible cats he used to buy us, he probably wouldn't have gone into that line of work at all," Granny said.

"True, my love. Shall we have lunch before we watch?"

Julian – lunchtime yesterday

"Have you always been interested in antiques?" the presenter of the daytime show asked.

"Oh yes, ever since I bought one for my grandparents when I was very young. It was a cat which they adored and over the years, I added more to their collection."

They chatted for a while about his career, allowing Julian to get in several mentions of the antiques business he was by then a partner of.

"And recently you made a very important find?" the presenter asked.

"Yes, the very last bed frame to be made by Parkers and sons before they stopped making furniture and turned their efforts to helping win WW1." It wasn't a valuable antique, but it was of historical importance, especially locally, as Parkers Engineering was one of the area's major employers.

As the television showed footage of Julian donating the bed frame to the local museum, where it would be restored and displayed thanks to financing by Parkers, Julian thought back to his grandparents' cat ornaments. It was hard to remember exactly what they'd been like, but he recalled how fond they'd always been of them and how sad they were to lose them in the burglary. He must make a real effort to find them some more.

<u>Granny and Grandad – Right after the show</u>

"Oh, didn't he look handsome?" Granny asked.

"He takes after me, I've always thought."

Granny looked at him in with what Grandad chose to consider was an admiring gaze.

"You don't think those awful ornaments he gave us when he was a kid were valuable, do you?" he asked.

"No chance of that! One was something the supermarket gave away at one time if people spent over a certain amount. I used to joke with my friends how we cut down on spending or did two trips so we wouldn't be landed with them. Two of the others were plastic, one was broken and badly glued back together."

"Were they really so awful? I thought we'd been pleased with the gifts?" Grandad had lost track over whether it was he or Granny who'd been right or wrong to be so enthusiastic about them.

"Yes, but bless him, he was such a little kid at the time and it was so sweet of him to get us anything. It was his thoughtfulness we appreciated."

"Ah, maybe I'll clear them out of the loft then."

"What are you talking about? They were stolen," Granny said.

"Actually they weren't. You remember how upset you were after the burglary, saying you'd nearly lost what was most precious to you? Well, I didn't know what that was but the cats were nowhere to be seen, so I guessed it wasn't them... "

"... you fool," Granny said.

"Sorry, love. I thought you disliked them as much as me."

"Oh, I did. It was you I meant... you dear, dear man. You're what's most precious to me and you could have been hurt and... " Granny went pink. Grandad guessed he did too.

"So what happened to the cats?" Granny asked.

"At first I really did think they'd been stolen, then I saw they'd just been knocked onto the floor. It seemed a good opportunity to put them out of sight, without hurting Julian's feelings, so I hid them in the loft. Do you think I did the right thing?"

"Of course you did," Granny said. "You always do."

6. Arts And Craftiness

Tell you the truth, I was feeling just a bit sorry for myself when I walked into that pub. I'd been to an art exhibition that afternoon, on the look out for someone rich and gullible, and seen the same pretty lass I'd noticed at a couple of previous shows. She never bought anything, and was too young for me, so I'd not have taken any notice except she reminded me of a girl I knew years back. What had her name been? There'd been so many I couldn't remember.

That's not what had unsettled me though. I'd overheard a couple talking about the legacy some painter had left. Got to thinking about mine and realised I had none. No family to carry on my genes and no one really knew about any of my achievements. Plus I was getting older.

For a while I wondered if I could change, do something else with my life. Something that'd make me proud. Pulled myself together though. I'd not done so badly for myself. Had a house and money in the bank and years ahead of me to enjoy what I'd worked for. All I needed was another little project to keep me interested.

My gaze flitted round the bar looking for a likely target. The same girl was there. I realised I'd been staring, but it was OK. She made eye contact and smiled. I'd still got it, the old power might have dimmed a little but it hadn't gone. Nah, who was I kidding? She was thirty, if that. Less than half my age. She wasn't interested in me that way, probably just thought she recognised me as a fellow art enthusiast.

Still, that didn't mean I couldn't use her interest to my advantage.

I've been able to live off women all my life. Know how to treat 'em see? Know what to say and when to keep quiet. Married the last one as she had lots of money and wasn't well. It was a good plan, but not perfect. She lived quite a while and spent a lot. Still, I inherited the house and a few quid when she died. I was pretty well set up. Lonely too. I'd been alone before but never felt it until she was gone.

The girl came over. "Hi, I'm sorry to bother you, but I don't know anyone here. I mean I don't know you either really, but ..."

I gave her my best reassuring smile, and let me tell you my best in that line is very good indeed. "But we're both admirers of Stephen Thomas' work?"

"Yes! Don't you just love what he does with the light? His 'Sunset at Stark Point' is just wonderful."

We chatted about his technique for a minute or two. I have a few stock phrases which get me through such situations.

"I'm Wendy by the way." She held out her hand.

I took it. "Giles."

"Oh that's a coincidence. I came here to meet someone called Giles." She pulled a piece of paper from her pocket. "Giles Cameron?"

What she held was far too small to be a warrant, but I was still wary.

"I was told he maybe had a room to let?" She sounded shy, but hopeful.

So, she needed somewhere to live. I hadn't thought of taking in a lodger, but it wasn't a bad idea if the money was right. "I'm Giles Cameron," I admitted wondering who'd put her on to me.

"I can pay my way," she assured me. "I've got a good job."

"So why would you be wanting to rent a room in a stranger's house?"

"Renting's so expensive isn't it? I mean for a house or a flat or something? Worse than a mortgage and I... I can't get one of those."

Bad credit rating? I wanted someone who'd hand their money over to me, not lose it all themselves.

Wendy studied her fingernails. "I don't have any savings left you see, for the deposit."

I had the feeling that if she'd looked up I'd have seen eyes full of tears.

"I did have. We did... My boyfriend invested my money, our money, in a scheme but it didn't work. He's gone." Her shoulders shook and she blew her nose. "He wrote that he's too embarrassed to face me. I'd tell him it doesn't matter, that I forgive him, but no one's seen him and a stranger answered his phone."

Crikey she was gullible if she'd fallen for that! It's an absolute classic! She did look sorry for herself though. I almost wanted to explain that he wasn't worth breaking her heart over, but didn't want to make her wary.

"You need a brandy or something, help you pull yourself together."

She nodded and I thought she wasn't going to take the hint, but eventually she opened her purse. "Would you get it? And something for yourself of course."

When I put our drinks and her change, every penny, on

the table she was calm again.

"Your friend Dave said that you were a widower and I thought I could help out round the house. I'd be glad to have something to do after work. I'm not a bad cook." She offered a hopeful little smile.

"I'm sure we can work something out."

She'd cook and clean and be company for me plus I'd get hold of that good salary. Sounded like I owed Dave a pint, but as I wasn't exactly sure which one of my acquaintances he was I couldn't pay up could I?

It worked a treat. As she'd said, she wasn't a bad cook. Once she saw how much I liked custard we had a pie or pudding smothered in it nearly every night.

"It's great to cook for someone who likes the same things as I do."

It wasn't just in food that we had the same tastes either. Often we'd sit and laugh at a film together or share our frustrations when City gave away another easy goal. She even put her hands to her head in the same way as I did when things got tense.

The girl was tidy too, almost obsessively so. The house was clean, my clothes too. She took care of everything, even the shopping. I helped her in return. Let her use my car and only charged her just enough to cover the running costs. Well, maybe a bit more. Then when my late wife's insurance ran out I had all the paperwork put in Wendy's name. A good deal; she took the train to work so I had it nine to five with no bills to pay. She had a good little runner, one careful lady owner and without the mark-up a garage would have put on it.

I kept Wendy safe from the chancers she seemed to

attract. Didn't want anyone else scamming her, did I? One was married I discovered and broke the news to her gently. If I couldn't warn her off them I got 'the lads' to warn them off her, if you catch my drift. Cost me a bit, but I saw it as an investment.

Yeah, me spending money on a woman. I let down my guard a bit, let her get close. I'd been so lonely and I liked her. Not like that, nothing nasty. She talked a lot and often mentioned her mother. Remember how I said she looked like a girl I once knew? Well I got thinking about it and reckoned that must have been getting on for about the time Wendy would have been born.

She was my daughter, I was almost sure of it. The thought did funny things to me. You see I've always had to keep a low profile, cover my tracks. I'd believed I'd leave the world with no trace I'd been in it, but it seemed I'd been wrong. In my spare room lived someone who might be my legacy.

I tried to find out for sure. If she was my daughter she'd look after me long into old age. I realised it needn't actually be true, just as long as she believed it was, so stopped looking for proof before I found out anything that wouldn't suit me. It was all going so well until Wendy told me she'd been offered a new job with much better pay.

"That's great news! We should go out and celebrate." No father could have been prouder. I even considered paying something towards the cost. Or offering to. Sometimes I forgot to take my wallet out with me.

"I'm not sure I'm going to take it yet."

"Why on earth wouldn't you?"

"It means moving away. I'd be on my own and… well, I'd miss you. I don't have any family anymore and…" Tears spilled down her face.

I patted her arm. "I'll come too. I could sell the house and we could buy somewhere together."

"You'd do that for me?"

"Yes. Didn't like to say before but I think maybe I'm your dad."

"You can't be."

I gave her the few details I could remember of the woman I thought was her mother.

"That does sound like her, but she told me about my father and you're nothing like the man she described. Well perhaps in looks a bit, but not in character."

"I met her in almost the same way I met you; at a gallery. She was an artist. Worked in pen and ink if I remember correctly?" I remember that because I'd briefly wondered if she'd be up for a bit of forgery.

"But… no… he was no good! A con artist who left Mum when she got pregnant! He made her miserable. You're not like that."

I hung my head in shame. I shouldn't have done it. I should have done what the man who took Wendy's savings did and left her mother with happy memories and kind thoughts, not made her bitter and miserable.

"I didn't really believe the child was mine. Didn't trust anyone back then. I've changed."

She was quiet for a while, then whispered, "Yes, I can see that. You've been kind to me."

I thought about it. I really had changed. I'd just blurted out what I thought was the truth and that wasn't like the old me at all. This new me didn't want to keep conning people, looking over his shoulder and moving on. He wanted to settle down and yes, do it with Wendy. He wasn't interested in romantic love now. All those years of pretence had soured him but he, I, would welcome the love of a daughter.

I knew I'd have problems sorting out all the paperwork over selling the house and buying a new one, because of all my name changes. Also I'm not that comfortable dealing with legalities and the people who make that their business. I confessed to Wendy.

"I'll help, but only if you promise those days are over."

I agreed with relief. "They are, I swear."

She squeezed my hand. "Don't worry, it'll all be fine… Dad."

It was so good to hear her call me that. Good as well to just do a straight deal over the house and not try to cheat anyone. We got a good price on the place my late wife had left me and Wendy picked out a lovely new home for us. Honesty was refreshing and simple. Too simple?

"You should come to the solicitor with me before you sign everything, just to make sure it's all OK," Wendy urged even before my doubts took hold.

The solicitor reassured and unnerved me in equal measures. He sat at a big solid desk in a big solid building, owned by a big solid legal firm. It was a relief that in my only dealings with them they were acting for, not against, me. He rambled on in legal jargon, warning us about the pitfalls of covenants and rights of way. Apparently a footpath lay behind our new garden and we'd not be allowed to breed pigs there. The high, strong wall and us not being farmers meant I wasn't concerned on either point.

For the first hour I was glad of the pot of tea we'd had before we came out. By the second I wished that I'd just had the one cup. The solicitor congratulated us on our prudence in avoiding tax and, spoken with his voice extra serious, death duties. I wasn't quite sure how we'd done that, but it was clearly good news. On and on he went. Should have worked for the police that man; I'd happily have signed a confession by the time he took the paperwork from his red leather file.

"Sorry, that was my fault," Wendy said in the lift afterwards. "I asked him to explain everything fully, but I'd no idea it would take so long."

Poor lass obviously didn't listen to much legal advice before she signed everything over to her swindling ex; I couldn't blame her for not wanting to make the same mistake.

"You did the right thing, love. Now let's find a café."

She ordered while I used the facilities, but I was back in time to pay for our coffee and cakes.

Wendy showed me pictures of the big modern kitchen and got me to think what I'd like her to cook for our first meal there. "I'll get us a take-away the first night as everything will be in boxes, but once it's all sorted I'll cook whatever you like."

"A roast, I think. Nothing says home cooking like Yorkshire puddings and proper gravy, but I'll get us that take-away, love."

Everything was packed up and in the removal lorry. As it drove off I thought what a good scam that would be; offer your services as a removal man and just drive off with some fool's furniture.

Wendy must have seen something in my face because she asked what I was smiling about.

After I told her she said, "You've given up all that kind of thing remember, Dad?"

I was nearly used to her calling me that and ready to start deserving it. I drove her to the hotel we'd booked for the night. Not quite sure when or why I'd suggested that but I was glad then that I had. Rather than dodge round men and furniture we'd arrive when everything was in place and we just had the small stuff the unpack. Wendy had checked their references carefully, I was sure we could trust them to do a good job.

In the morning I waited for Wendy in reception.

"Would you care to settle the bill, sir?" the woman on the desk asked.

Why not? I thought. It was the start of my new life and besides I'd want Wendy grateful to me rather than thinking I wasn't pulling my weight and ought to do the decorating or something. I couldn't find my credit card, but that was nothing new. I had just about enough cash on me to cover it.

"There's a letter for you," the woman said as she printed my receipt.

I didn't see how there could be, but that didn't stop her handing me an envelope with my name on the front. The handwriting was Wendy's. It contained a father's day card. That day had been and gone, but I supposed she too was considering this a fresh start. Perhaps she wanted to show it wasn't too late for us. The picture on the front was a cartoon of a man not too unlike how I'd presented myself a few years back. It said, 'Dad, you're funny, clever and good looking …' inside it said 'which explains where I got it all from!' I liked that. Anything about me being a good father wouldn't have been appropriate, but that made me laugh.

As I waited I reflected that nice as the card was, even that jokey comment wasn't really true. Her looks and personality had come from her mother. Her sharp intelligence, yes maybe I could take the credit there. My own good points though, well I'd got them from her. She'd taught me to be honest, trusting and to care.

I waited and waited. Wendy didn't come and I began to worry. First I went up to her room, wondering if she was ill in bed but the chambermaid was in there stripping off the sheets. Next I looked in the car park. There was no sign of her vehicle. All sorts of ideas went through my head. She'd been kidnapped by someone I'd wronged in the past or she'd gone off to buy me a gift to go along with the card and got hurt on the way. Or there was a problem with the new house and she'd rushed off to sort it out and had an accident. Those were things I could never have forgiven myself for.

It took a while but eventually I realised why she wasn't there, wasn't answering her phone and had left no message other than that card. She had left of her own free will and didn't want me with her. The full implications of that took longer to sink in. A walk to the bank, explanation about having mislaid my card and proving my identity revealed that by then my savings were gone. The few coins in my pocket, Wendy's card and the contents of my overnight bag were all I possessed.

Another trudge, this time to the estate agent's, proved I wasn't half owner of the house I thought Wendy and I had bought together.

"It's still on the market if you're interested?"

No not sold to Miss Wilkins. Client confidentiality meant they couldn't tell me which house she had bought, if she'd bought one at all.

"But we bought it together," I tried to explain.

"No, sir. You viewed a property together, but your name doesn't appear on any purchase documents."

Eventually I got out of them that I'd signed a power of attorney giving Wendy control of everything including the money I'd got from selling my old place. My confusion and dismay probably convinced them she'd been absolutely right to do so.

I stumbled away and eventually found myself back in the art gallery where I'd first seen Wendy. With the last coins in my pocket I bought a postcard of the painting she'd admired back then. I sat and stared at it, but it was Wendy's skill I was admiring, not the artist's. Of course she'd searched me out and manipulated me from the start. Until then I'd not been absolutely sure Wendy really was my child, but now I have no doubts. I'd been scammed by my own flesh and blood, the daughter I'd come to love and who is my legacy to the world.

I'm so proud of her.

7. The Amateur Gravedigger

You read stories of sweet old ladies burying their awful husbands in the garden. That can make a fun story if it seems he deserved it. If he was anything like my Freddie, I'm guessing a lot of readers would feel he did deserve it.

A nice fantasy that; kill him off, bury him quick and get on with your life. No more taunts. No more shouting. No more being scared in your own home. There's just one snag – it's not as easy as it's often made out to be.

So often the new widow takes the body to the woods. You've heard the term 'dead weight' I expect? It has the reputation of meaning hard to shift with good reason. And if you did manage to get the recently deceased into the woods unseen, you'd be a long way from finished.

Even in the back garden, where there are no tree roots, my arms were tiring within minutes. After an hour I was exhausted and blistered, but not halfway done. I hadn't planned on a grave of traditional dimensions. Just big enough to squeeze him in, and deep enough that nobody would accidentally make contact with skin and bone as they planted a tray of marigolds. I'm reasonably fit and not yet 40. No way could a little old lady dig a hole big enough to bury a man on her own all in one go.

Professionals, using a mechanical digger, take a couple of hours. I know because I've seen them in the churchyard as I've walked Bruno. Having only three legs, doesn't mean a dog doesn't like plenty of exercise. Strictly speaking, Bruno was Freddie's dog, but Bruno didn't know that. It was me who fed and brushed him. Me who cleaned up after him, took him for walks and all the rest.

It wasn't just Freddie and Bruno I looked after. Freddie had other animals over the years, all taken in from shelters. The ugly ones, or those needing extra care, the old ones who'd not be with us for long. Those no one else wanted. People said how kind he was. How generous.

He said that's why he'd married me – because with my scar no one else would ever want me. That whatever attention he paid me would be better than nothing. Worse thing was he convinced me it was true.

At first it wasn't too bad. Whilst I was still pathetically grateful that he'd rescued me from my single state, and the pity of friends and family, he was rarely angry. But it's hard to show constant gratitude for a life which doesn't make you happy.

The animals are partly why I put up with it. I loved them. Especially Bruno. Freddie did too, as much as he was able to love anyone or anything. He stopped yelling at me so much when he saw it distressed Bruno. He shut the dog in another room when he knew his words or actions would reduce me to tears.

The last animal Freddie brought home was a kitten with burn marks. The scars on the poor little thing were so red and sore. They'd have reminded me of my own, even without Freddie saying how ugly we both were. I was better off than the kitten though. My scar was fading and I could hide it behind a long fringe. It was stupid of me to say so to Freddie, to show I was gaining a little confidence.

He said he'd blacken my eye, see if I had enough hair to cover that too. I don't know now if he really would have, but I believed it at the time. Instead of begging him not to, I said I wouldn't cover the evidence. I'd let the world see what he was really like. Well, his mother and a divorce lawyer at any rate.

Maybe it was the shock of me finally standing up to him which caused his fatal heart attack? Maybe the lazy, greedy, angry man already had it coming? Anyway, he died and he's buried in the churchyard. I watched them digging his grave as I walked by with Bruno.

You didn't think I was burying Freddie in the garden, did you? If I'd done that I couldn't have claimed the insurance money and kept feeding the animals. No, it's Bruno. Dear, dear Bruno. He died two years after Freddie. For now it's just me and the kitten, although of course she's grown into a cat. Not a beautiful one, but still deserving of love. Just like me.

8. On-line Lies

Names say a lot, so I won't tell you mine. Roger Rolex is what I'm using in the chat-rooms now. Previously, I've been Jason2Jags and Multi-mill-malc. Every new operation requires another name. It will change again once I've got what I want and moved on to new prey.

My current target is Eloise Jones. Eloise; exotic, full of promise. It could mean anything, but actually means nothing. I looked it up, 'of unknown origin'. I looked up Jones too; it's derived from Johns, which is derived from something else, which was translated from the Latin name of a saint, or perhaps an apostle. A good name to hide behind.

She doesn't know I know her real name. We chat on-line where she's known as Connie. That sounds innocent, sweet. Her chat-room ID shows a photograph, a real one, of herself. I don't use a photo and I'm careful what I say. I don't want to be traced. Maybe, like sweet Connie, you think you're careful too? It's amazing how much you reveal. Referring to where you went at the weekend or the company you work for can help someone determined to track you down. Someone like me.

I've been watching 'Connie' for a while now. She hasn't seen me – I'm very careful. I know where she lives; I've photographed her sunbathing in the garden. I know who she speaks to; sometimes I've been close enough to hear what she says.

Connie wasn't shy with personal information. She didn't mind chatting to men about her long blonde hair, curvaceous figure and lonely life. Naturally I was interested. To be honest she sounded almost desperate. Desperate enough to be interested in a man like me. She liked money, that much was obvious. I played on her loneliness and mercenary streak. I flirted a little, I mentioned how my soft top sports car was wasted on my bald head, that her silky locks would look much more charming streaming in the breeze. I always told her when I'd be away, skiing or sailing, in case I couldn't get on-line.

She believed every word. The silly girl asked her other on-line friends. She wasn't to know that a change of user name and a few less spelling mistakes turned me from Roger Rolex into Shopping Babe. My alter ego confided to Connie that she'd met me. Her online report; *'nice enough guy, but obsessed about his money. I expected a Rolex from this name, but not one for everyday of the week! You might think from my name that I loves to shop, but honey, let me tell you that spending money can lose it's appeal. The guy doesn't have much else going for him and he's not exactly the smartest!'*

Strangely, Connie didn't lose interest. She began discussing the stock market, bonds and investment opportunities. I played my part well. It was easy, I've done it before. The girls don't resist and they never get to tell their story, so I'm free to capture another and another.

The flirting continued for a while. I dropped hints, but let her make the first move. I always do. They're less suspicious if they're the one setting the trap. Once the girl has said she'd like to meet, I warn her to be careful – doesn't she want to check me out first? 'No need' she says. Doesn't mention the chat with Shopping Babe, but I can't complain. It's not as though I'm being totally honest. I tell her we'll meet in a public place. That makes her feel safe. I name somewhere expensive, somewhere I won't be recognised.

I'm quite excited as I prepare to meet her. She'll be there I'm sure. That's all I need. I'll buy her a drink; they always let you buy them a drink. Soon she'll be relaxed, very relaxed. I'll have control then, she won't get away.

I put the orchid in my buttonhole, just as we'd arranged. The champagne and glasses are on the table when she arrives. I pour a glass for her as she sits opposite.

I offer a toast, "To Connie, even more beautiful in person than on-line." She smiles, tastes her drink. We talk. Soon the conversation moves to money. Honestly, I cannot say which of us steered it in that direction. She repeats what she said on-line, sipping her drink delicately between sentences. Soon it's enough.

"Eloise Jones," I say. "I am arresting you for attempt to defraud. You do not have to say anything now, but it may harm your defence ..."

9. Flight Of Fancy

Clarissa was excited, sitting in the back of the taxi starting a journey which would change her life. Nervous too; she was taking a risk travelling out to a man she'd met on the internet. Still she knew Kirk wasn't after her money and they'd chatted to each other lots of times.

Thanks to her job in a retirement home, Clarissa was good at judging people just from speaking to them on the phone as they made enquiries into the health of residents. Sometimes the family genuinely cared and had good reason for not coming in person. Usually though they just phoned to ease their conscience or check how soon they'd inherit. One man, when told his great aunt, Muriel Fletcher, was suffering dementia insisted that if she didn't know where she was he wanted her moved into a smaller, cheaper room. Clarissa said none were available. It wasn't true, but moving Muriel would have caused her great distress.

Poor dear thought she was back at her boarding school. Muriel had a friend called Clarinda back then and sometimes thought her young carer was the same person. Clarissa indulged her in that fantasy. They'd gossiped together about books and music popular in the forties and about boys, although Clarissa was careful to tone down her amorous encounters to suit a listener from a more innocent time.

Her employer allowed her to take a bottle of sweet sherry in to Muriel, saying an occasional glass wouldn't hurt.

Clarissa pretended she'd smuggled it past the teachers. They sipped the drink between giggles and behind a closed door. At Christmas Clarissa gave Muriel a box of candied fruit.

"Oh thank you, my dear! But you already gave me that pretty brooch."

Clarissa realised she was being mistaken for Clarinda again, so played along by saying she deserved an extra treat.

"And so do you! Now what could I give you? Help me up a minute will you, dear?"

With Clarissa's assistance, Muriel rummaged through her sideboard until she found the jewellery box. "Have these, Clarry dear. They'll look lovely against your skin. I'm too pale for them." She gave Clarissa a set of oddly shaped beads.

Maybe they'd been fashionable when Muriel was a girl as she didn't seem the type to give her friends rubbish. "Thank you, they're very pretty."

"Aren't they? Wish I could remember where I got them."

Clarissa guessed Muriel's husband had given them to her but as, in Muriel's mind, she hadn't yet met him she couldn't say so.

It wasn't until weeks later that Clarissa learned more about both Mr Fletcher and the beads. By then Clarissa had 'met' Kirk and soon had other things on her mind.

When Clarissa gently tried to explain she was going away, Muriel was excited.

"Lucky you going to the Isle of Wight again! Oh how I wish I could come with you like last year."

Thinking of her work had taken Clarissa's mind off her journey, but once at the airport it was time to concentrate on the future. She paid the taxi driver and took her small bag and one case into Manchester airport. She just had to get through the next few hours and she'd be with Kirk and everything would be OK.

Clarissa fiddled with her necklace and looked around at her fellow travellers. Was her hand luggage small enough? It must be, she'd measured it twice to be sure it complied with the dimensions Kirk sent. Her suitcase was definitely light enough; there was hardly anything in it. She'd not wanted to pack: soon she'd be able to buy much better clothes, but Kirk had insisted she look just like any other traveller to get through all the checks.

She'd packed a few items which once belonged to people she'd cared for at work. Sometimes grateful residents actually left things to the staff. Other times they just picked through what was left after the families had collected the good stuff. What they didn't want went to the charity shop. Clarissa, once she'd planned this trip, had taken several sets of clothing.

She wore one of the jackets for her flight, so the clothes would seem as though they belonged to her, were anyone to examine them. She pushed her hand deep into a pocket and felt something small and smooth, almost like a sea polished pebble. No problem, smooth solid objects were allowed on planes. It was anything sharp or liquid that was suspect. Clarissa had read a few scaremongering reports which suggested mothers carrying milk for their babies were liable to a strip search and that a nail file could be classified as a deadly weapon by an over zealous official. She panicked and didn't pack any liquids at all, not even her mascara. Of course, by tomorrow she'd be able to buy anything she wanted, Kirk would see to that.

She confirmed she'd packed the case herself and handed over her ticket and passport. She'd got it years ago for a school trip to France. The picture didn't really look much like her now but she was nodded quickly through. Her final hurdle, on the British side of the departure gate, was the body scanner.

"Please put any metal items in here," a stern looking, female security official said, holding a dish which looked very like the ones used at work for residents who felt sick.

Clarissa had nothing and said so.

"Your necklace?"

"It's not real gold, just plastic." She tapped a fingernail against it to make her point. What she'd said was true, the thick chain which formerly belonged to a resident from the home really was plastic. When she first got it, it had glass stones in lots of different colours. Clarissa had changed them for clear ones. It was pretty, if you didn't look too closely. Clarissa suppressed a giggle as it occurred to her the lack of deodorant should deter anyone from wanting to get too close.

Finally Clarissa was permitted to proceed to the departure lounge. She gave a small sigh of relief and went in search of a bookstore for something to help pass the time on the flight. Soon she'd always select the latest hardbacks, not look for something in the reduced bin.

Clarissa enjoyed the nine hour flight more than she'd expected. The food wasn't at all bad, the book was amusing and when she wasn't eating or reading she daydreamed about how much fun her life would be once she'd met up with Kirk in America.

Orlando airport was more like a nightmare than a dream. Passengers had to queue for almost two hours, without seats or water, even for the elderly. If residents where Clarissa had worked were treated like that she'd have been prosecuted for neglect!

"Welcome to the United States of America. Enjoy your visit," the official finally said as though daring Clarissa to have fun.

Never mind, all she had to do now was find a taxi to take her to the hotel where Kirk was waiting. That was easily and quickly accomplished.

Clarissa knocked on the door of room 326 and waited for her first sight of Kirk. The man who opened the door looked … ordinary. No wonder he'd found it difficult to describe himself. He was neither tall nor short, he was of average build with nondescript, greying hair.

"Excuse me, can you direct me to the nearest arboretum?" she asked.

His smile made him look quite nice as he gave his reply to the code phrase she'd greeted him with.

"Sorry about all the cloak and dagger stuff," he said. "I hope you didn't have any trouble on the flight?"

"No, everything went smoothly."

"Good. Now if you don't mind, I'd like to see what I'm getting for my money."

Clarissa stood perfectly still as he stepped closer, lifted his arms and placed his hands gently around her neck. Kirk undid her necklace and prised out the diamonds she'd rescued before Muriel Fletcher's great nephew could get his hands on them.

"Just as you said and here, just as I said," he handed her a huge bundle of money.

Clarissa counted it and left, doubting anyone would guess

she was carrying a million dollars as she flew home. She grinned all the way back, partly because of the champagne she treated herself to and partly because she'd been right to trust Kirk after he'd given an online valuation of the gems and offered to buy them, no questions asked and no paperwork needed. Clarissa settled into her seat and let her hand slide back into her jacket pocket. It had been worth selling the antique pearls Muriel had given her at Christmas to finance the flight, but she was glad she'd kept one for herself.

Muriel would get her holiday to the Isle of Wight, in fact it would last however long the poor old girl had left. Clarissa would care for her and then keep whatever was left of the cash. A plan she was sure the older woman would have agreed to had she realised the diamonds had gone missing from her jewellery box.

10. The Impossible Selfie

Martine's phone played a burst of Pretty Woman and she snatched it up eagerly. "Hi, Sis. How's things?"

"Really, really good. Just going out for the day actually," Ella replied.

"You don't half get a lot of time off work," Martine said.

"Didn't I say? I left."

"But you loved it!"

"Yeah, but like Toby said, I don't need to work and so many other people do."

"I suppose… "

"Sorry, gotta go – Toby's waiting. Laters!"

Martine sighed. It had been too long since she'd had a proper chat with Ella. Phone calls were usually cut short because Ella's husband wanted attention and he was always there when they met in person. As they were newlyweds that was understandable, but the sisters, who had no other family, had always been very close. Martine couldn't help feeling she'd been pushed aside.

Martine grew increasingly uneasy during the morning. Ella had sounded too cheerful – the way people can when they're trying to convince themselves they're happy. Toby was very romantic, often surprising Ella with dinners out or trips to London. Those often occurred when she'd planned to spend time with Martine, or friends, but it apparently never occurred to Ella to say no to him. If he wanted her attention she'd immediately abandon whatever she was doing or whoever she was speaking to. Now she'd quit work at his suggestion. Did he bully her?

Pretty Woman played again. Martine was about to speak when she realised it was just a message. She opened it to see a headshot of her sister. In it Ella's strawberry blonde hair was beautifully fanned out in water, but she had her eyes closed and looked sad. That wasn't right. Ella's usual selfies were carefully posed and she tended to either do that silly pout or be grinning madly.

Martine called her sister, but was informed 'this person's phone has been switched off'. That too was very unlike Ella. She might only say, "Sorry, can't talk now, I'll call you back," but she always answered. Maybe for once Toby was letting her drive and she'd switched it off so she wasn't distracted?

Martine tried to ignore the feeling of dread which was creeping up her spine and told herself Ella was playing their old game. Martine used to photograph a detail of a new purchase and send it to Ella so she could guess what she'd bought. Ella would text 'see you at seven' and attach a picture clue as to where they were to meet. The last time they'd played, Ella had sent nothing but a selfie. It had taken Martine quite a while to notice the engagement ring.

If this was a clue, what was Ella trying to say? There was nobody else to be seen and nothing much in the background except water. The sea probably. Did Toby want them to move to the coast? Get a holiday home by a beach? If Ella was moving permanently then Martine would follow. Thanks to the legacy left to the two girls that would be no problem.

Martine kept trying to call, with no luck. Why would Ella

be in the sea? She'd never been much of a swimmer even in tropical waters, and she didn't look warm. Actually she looked really, really cold. It wasn't impossible that Ella had taken a selfie with her eyes closed, but if she had there'd be a reason. Maybe Ella had a good reason for not answering her phone. Even so Martine was worried.

She rang Toby's number. At first it seemed his phone would also go unanswered.

Eventually she heard his voice. "Hello, Martine."

"Are you OK? You sound odd."

"It's Ella… "

"Something bad has happened, hasn't it?"

"I'm afraid so."

"Where is she?"

"I don't think it…"

"Please, Toby, just tell me where she is."

Martine put the location into her sat nav and drove straight over. The tiny car park at the top of the cliff contained Toby's car, two police vehicles, a coastguard van, ropes and other rescue equipment, and an ambulance. A covered stretcher was being loaded into that. A few locks of wet strawberry blonde hair hung over one side.

Someone screamed. It wasn't until one of the ambulance crew calmed her down that Martine realised she'd made the sound herself. "No! No, no, no." She kept saying it, but couldn't drown out the news that her wonderful sister was gone. She'd fallen from the cliff into the sea and rocks below.

"She was trying to take a selfie when part of the path gave way," Toby said. "If only she'd stayed with me and not gone ahead."

Martine was suddenly angry. "How dare you blame her! Of course she needed to get away from you to use her phone. You've cut her off from all her friends and tried to do the same with me. She died trying to escape your control, and call me!"

He looked so shocked Martine regretted her outburst. The poor man had just lost his wife.

"Your sister called you this morning?" a police officer asked Martine.

"Yes. And later sent the strangest message."

"When was this?"

"About an hour ago."

"That's impossible," Toby said, very forcefully.

Martine agreed with him. There was the fact it was announced with the tune which played when Ella rang, despite it just being a message. More unsettling it seemed the picture must have been taken about the time of Ella's death. Toby didn't know that though. What if the shock she'd seen on his face, when she first mentioned a message, wasn't grief but fear?

"No it isn't. You said she went on ahead. Ella could fire off a text in seconds, the only way you could know she hadn't was if you were right by her side."

He stepped toward her, a horrible expression distorting his usual good looks.

"You were, weren't you, Toby? You never let Ella out of your sight."

"I had no choice. You were always trying to push your way between us, reminding her that you're all the family she had. You even got her to change her will so you got everything instead of me!"

61

"What? No, I…"

"There's no point denying it. I've seen it!"

So Martine had been right, Ella wasn't as happy as she'd tried to sound. "No doubt she had her reasons, but …"

"Oh yes, she had reasons. But bad luck, it hasn't been signed. I checked her email and found she was going to do that today, so arranged a surprise trip." Toby made a horrible sound, almost like a child's giggle. "You're not the only one who can push!"

The police officers stepped forward so they were one each side of Toby. "Tobias Gould, we are arresting you on suspicion of murder. You do not have to say anything … "

As he was led away, Martine's phone again played a burst of Pretty Woman. Again there was no call, just a message containing an impossible selfie of Ella. In it she looked peaceful and had her hand raised as though waving goodbye.

11. Making Him Say Yes

Monday morning at eight I walked up the path and knocked on his door. It took him a long time to answer. When he did, he seemed kind of surprised to see me.

I asked, "Will you marry me?"

"No," he said and shut the door. Shut me out.

Tuesday, he wouldn't answer when I knocked. And knocked. And knocked.

I waited down the street. Saw him walk briskly towards me. Watched as his pace slowed then sped up as he neared me.

"Do you love me?" I asked as he drew level.

"No." He rushed away. Too briskly for me to keep up without running. That would have been undignified, so I watched him go. He didn't look back. Not once.

Wednesday, a car pulled up outside his house. He ran down the steps and jumped in. Don't know why. It wasn't raining. In order to speak to him, I had to go to his office. I don't think he'd expected to see me there.

"Will you take me out, tonight?" I asked as he gaped from behind his terminal.

"No."

Thursday, the girl on reception told me to take a seat. I waited. And waited. And waited. And waited.

At five thirty he raced past.

"Will you kiss me?"

"No," he shouted. He shouted at me!

Friday, I waited again. Waited until they locked up and I had to leave.

Maybe he was sick?

Saturday, very early, I smashed his window. Found him in his bed. He looked startled, but not ill. I saw the truth then. He'd not been ill on the Friday, he'd been avoiding me.

I had to make him see he cared, so I held broken glass against my throat. "You hate me, don't you? Wish I'd die?"

"Yes."

It wasn't the answer I wanted.

Police, doctors, the judge, Mum, they all say I shouldn't ask him anything else. They're wrong. He said yes once, he'll say it again.

12. Is The Cold War Over?

"Why did he do that, Gran?" Aron, from his position in the back seat, spoke almost into her ear.

"Do what, love?" Valerie's concentration was more on joining the busy roundabout than his words.

"He parked beside us as we were getting into your car, but instead of going into the sport's centre he drove out again."

The boy had her full attention now. She too had noticed the car pull up next to them. There had been something vaguely familiar about the driver. It unsettled Valerie that she couldn't be sure whether or not she'd really seen him before. She was losing her old skills.

"Maybe he forgot something?" Valerie suggested, trying to keep her voice light.

"Big scary man must live near us," Judi added.

Valerie checked her rearview mirror again. Sure enough the registration plate contained the letters BSM. Making up names for drivers or their vehicles based on the registration letters was a game she'd suggested a year ago. For them it was a way to help them learn about words, but Valerie once used the technique to aid her memory.

"What's wrong, Gran?" Aron had asked the first time she drove the children further than to the school gates. For a moment him calling her Gran had made her so happy she thought she'd be able to forget the fears that had been so important when she'd worked for MI6. The children lived next door. Their real grandparents were miles away and visited rarely, Valerie had no one and so the family sort of adopted her.

Valerie hadn't wanted to lie to Aron and Judi but she could hardly say she was checking if Russians were attempting to kidnap her, or Middle Eastern terrorists planned to kill her. Of course they wouldn't be. The cold war was over and no Russians would want to extract the secrets she'd long forgotten. There were still terrorists, but different ones to the enemies she'd made. So she told the truth.

"I was wondering if we are being followed." She made a game of it, encouraging the children to look at the cars behind and guess where they were going and why. Valerie didn't drive fast, not with her precious 'grandchildren' in the car so few vehicles stayed behind them for long.

"That trailer has got ponies in for a princess to ride," Judi guessed.

"That tractor is going to plant something that aliens will make crop circles in," Aron informed her.

Just as Valerie used to when she was working they made up the names from the registration letters. Then as now it helped to remember the details and be sure it really was the same vehicle. She was delighted when Judi decided IRA stood for 'in red anorak' and Aron thought PLO could mean 'paints large objects' because the van was decorated by hand. The work she'd once done had helped allow these children to grow up in safety and peace.

"Are you sure it was Big Scary Man who parked next to us?" she asked.

"Yes, Gran. I made it up from the letters but he really

does look big, " Judi explained. "Is he really scary?" she wanted to know.

So did Valerie. Without indicating she made a sudden left hand turn. BSM followed. If he was really going home for something he'd forgotten he must also have forgotten where he lived until Valerie had turned.

Although they did their best none of them could come up with a plausible explanation for the man still being behind them after a couple more erratic turns on Valerie's part. She drove straight to the police station. If the man was up to no good that might make him change his mind and if not at least there would be help at hand.

"Stay in the car children," she instructed before getting out herself.

The man, who was indeed large and scary looking, approached. He carried an odd shaped bundle against his body. There could be anything in that.

"I caught up with you at last," he stated in a strong Russian accent.

Valerie nodded, standing her ground.

"You dropped this," he said holding the bundle which she now saw was the wet towels she'd wrapped around her and the children's bathing suits.

As Valerie thanked him she realised where she'd seen him before. He was one of the lifeguards at the sport's centre. Valerie felt all the tension ease from her body. Until then she'd not truly believed the past was behind her but the proof was right in front of her. She may have been enemies of this man's father and uncles but she knew she could trust him to keep her, and the children, safe.

13. Knowing Jane

I hadn't been looking forward to my brother-in-law's visit, but answered his call with as much enthusiasm as I could muster.

"Sorry, Graham," he said. "I'm not sure I'm going to make it over to you today."

Since his wife requested a trial separation Bill's called in on us whenever his work allowed. His stated reason was to cheer Jane and I up now we're retired but, as he was a bit self-centred, time in his company generally had the opposite effect.

"Don't worry," I said, trying to hide my relief. "Jane's out anyway."

"Did she forget I was coming?"

"She asked me to say she's sorry to miss you. She's gone for a spa day."

"Are you sure? That doesn't sound like her."

"Of course I'm sure." I know my Jane and this sudden change of plan was just typical of her.

I'd just started scarifying the lawn when Bill arrived. "I managed to make time to see you after all," he said. That was closely followed by, "What on earth are you doing?"

It was a fair question as it initially makes the grass look worse rather than better. I tried explaining, but gave up when he mentioned plastic grass as an alternative.

After that our conversation became ever more awkward. Ordinarily I'd have stopped what I was doing and invited him in for a drink or snack, but as he appeared short of time, and I wasn't eager to talk to him, I hadn't done that. Bill seemed to be trying to make some sort of point, but I didn't know what. He kept asking if everything was OK between Jane and me. You know how it is, the more you say 'yes of course' the less convincing it sounds.

"And you're coping OK with retirement?" he asked.

"Yes. Enjoying it actually, especially having time for the garden."

"And Jane? She has her interests, I suppose?"

"Yes, she does."

"Music of course is very important to her."

It isn't, as surely her brother knew. I wondered if this was some kind of test. "Not particularly," and then because he'd been there some time and didn't look ready to leave, "Would you like a coffee?"

"Yes please. And I'll just use your bathroom if I may?"

Perhaps that request explained why he'd seemed so uncomfortable, but I Googled dementia tests, to see if that's what he was up to. Bill wasn't gone as long as I'd anticipated. Feeling flustered and a touch guilty, I pulled open the fridge door to hide what I was doing. Then it occurred to me that if he saw me apparently taking my phone from the fridge he really would be worried about me. I shoved it in next to the cheese and took out the milk.

I was uncomfortable waiting for the kettle to boil and almost dropped the sugar cannister when I heard a ringing sound. I tried to ignore the expression on Bill's face as I fetched my phone from behind the Cheddar and tried to answer a non existent call.

"It's the doorbell," he told me.

"Excuse me," I said grateful for the distraction.

The new visitor was Tony, a chap I used to work with. To be honest we were never close in our working days, but my Jane always got on well with his wife at company functions, so we stayed in touch. Jane and I had them over for a meal or went to them about once a month. Lately those evenings have been a bit tense.

"Hi, lovely to see you!" I said with perhaps a shade too much enthusiasm.

"Just passing. Decided to call in," he said. "See how you're doing."

Something in his manner seemed odd, but I thought it was just Bill who'd got me on edge. "I was just going to make coffee. Fancy one?"

"Please."

When we reached the kitchen Bill had taken over the coffee making. I introduced the pair of them, then Bill asked Tony if he took milk and sugar.

"Just milk, thanks," Tony gave him a big smile. Then to me he said, "Didn't realise you had guests staying. That explains it!"

"I'm not staying and I'm on my own," Bill said, pointedly.

I wasn't sure if that's because he felt I shouldn't be left unattended, or he was about to get started on his separation again. Not wanting either conversation I quickly asked, "Explains what?"

"Saw Jane food shopping yesterday," Tony said, as though convinced that was her cover for selling secrets to the Russians or drug dealing.

"Getting something for our tea, I expect."

Tony's expression was a pretty good match for Bill's when I'd retrieved my phone from the fridge. Maybe I'd been over enthusiastic raking the lawn and had moss hanging from my ears or something. I went to the bathroom to check. Nothing seemed to be amiss until I returned to the kitchen. The abrupt silence suggested my guests had been talking about me.

"Where is Jane by the way?" Tony asked.

"At a spa, having a total body makeover," I explained.

"Right. Um, you're absolutely sure about that, are you?"

"Of course I'm sure." Did he think I'd bumped her off or something? I showed him my slightly chilled phone. "There's Jane and our granddaughter having face packs." They both had green goo, so bright it probably glowed in the dark, slathered over them – something I intended to tease Jane about later. Tony and Bill both had a look.

"Could be anyone," Tony said.

"I know my Jane and that's her."

"Doesn't seem her kind of thing," Tony said.

"That's right, she never wore makeup even as a teenager," Bill said. "Why has she started now?"

"That's just the kind of person she is," I said.

"And why this sudden interest in music?" Bill demanded.

"Same answer."

"Why was she buying steaks?" Tony asked.

That they were for us to eat seemed so obvious I hesitated before saying it. Tony clearly thought there was more to it. Jane hadn't mentioned seeing him. The sudden news about the spa trip explained that, but not why Tony felt the need to call today to see how we were. If they'd talked, he should have known the answer – so something had caused him concern.

Bill's behaviour was a bit strange too. He doesn't often take an interest in anything not connected with himself or what's on his mind. All that had been on his mind recently was the trouble his marriage was in. Oh!

"You think my wife is having an affair?" I asked.

The look on both their faces confirmed it.

"I know my Jane and she definitely isn't."

"You never know with women," Bill said. "This sudden interest in music and makeup must mean something."

"And buying meat when you're vegetarians."

"Ah! No, Tony, we're not vegetarians. We're happy to eat that way at your home and avoid meat meals when you come to us, because we don't want to cause offence by eating it in front of you. Maybe Jane looked a bit embarrassed for having it in her trolley when she met you for the same reason?"

"Could be it, I suppose."

"And Bill, your wife adores the opera and doesn't like to go alone. When Jane found out she offered to go with her. It's the same with this spa day. Our granddaughter very much wanted to go and the friend who was due to accompany her, and do the driving, had to cancel at the last minute, so Jane offered to take her place."

"But she doesn't like those things."

"No, but she likes to make people happy." And then, because I knew there was something Jane felt should be said, but couldn't bring herself to utter, I added, "Bill, if you were more like your sister and did things simply to make your wife happy, maybe she'd come back to you. And Tony, you could do with being a bit more like me, and trust the woman you love."

Both Bill and Tony looked uncomfortable at that. Jane won't enjoy that bit when I tell her, but she'll be pleased at the possibility the conversation might save one marriage and improve another. You see, I know my Jane and that's what she's like.

14. Discovering Hidden Treasure

"How'd it go, Pet?" Karl asked his daughter as she skipped into the house, followed by her mother.

"Brilliant! Miss Olsson says I'll pass Grade six soon. With my new shoes I'll do even better, I know I will." She performed a pirouette.

Karl met his wife's gaze. "Of course you will." He'd have to find the money for her ballet shoes somehow, just as he'd scrimped and scraped for her lessons. There must be something else he and Lynne could cut back on.

"What's up, Dad?"

"Nothing, sweetie. Is it Let's Dance tonight?" Maybe they could sell the TV. That might bring enough money in, and Petunia could watch the few programmes she enjoyed at a friend's house. He and Lynne hardly had time to watch after working all the hours they could and acting as a taxi service for their daughter.

"Yes, but there's an antiques thing on," Petunia said. "You watch that and I'll record Let's Dance for later."

Karl and Lynne settled down to watch and enjoy the drink and sandwich Petunia made for them, before she went up to her room to do her homework.

"She's a good lass," Karl said. "Wish we could do more for her."

"We do what we can and it's a lot more than some get."

Karl nodded. What she said was true, but Petunia enjoyed

far fewer advantages than he'd enjoyed at that age. He'd gone to a private school, had a pony, all the latest toys. Everything was paid for by the money Granddad had earned from his antiques business. His children, Karl's mother included, inherited plenty of cash, but no interest in the business. Just a few years after Granddad's death, the money ran out.

Almost all Karl had now were happy memories of Granddad and an interest in antiques. He'd bought a few nice things at car boot sales to decorate their home. It would be great to learn one of them was really valuable, but it wasn't very likely.

Karl had been fascinated by the items in Granddad's shop and learned quite a bit from him. Maybe that's why he'd been Granddad's favourite. Karl could still recall how impressed Granddad had been when he was learning to write. Karl had showed him the page where he'd carefully copied his teacher's neat writing and then flipped over to where his mum had written more words for him to practice writing.

"Want to do some more, boy?" Granddad had asked.

When Karl eagerly accepted, Granddad wrote word after word. "Take your time, boy. Write it out just like mine."

Karl was rewarded for his neat lines of letters. A big bar of chocolate, sheet of stickers or pack of stink bombs. Later he wrote new words, replicating the letters in different handwriting samples Granddad gave him.

When the old man died, he left Karl his writing desk, complete with old sheets of paper and a couple of bottles of ink. Karl also inherited the stuffed swan he'd long ago affectionately named Cedric. Dark wood hadn't suited Karl and Lynne's house and the swan now looked rather tatty so both were placed in the attic and all but forgotten.

Karl's attention wandered between memories of helping his grandfather in the shop and the television screen. The presenter was talking about a desk. A Chippendale in perfect condition. Not surprisingly it was valued at an incredibly high figure. Granddad's desk was almost as old and in almost as good condition, but the maker was nowhere near as famous.

Why hadn't he thought of selling Granddad's desk before? It wasn't worth nearly as much as the Chippendale, but probably fairly valuable. Karl was never going to use it and surely Granddad would approve of him encouraging his great-granddaughter's talent? Karl didn't wait for the programme to end before climbing up into the attic.

Karl carefully removed the contents and placed them into boxes. As he did so he again came across the cigar clipper and remembered puzzling over it when he'd first got the desk. Granddad had never smoked. He studied it more carefully than he'd done then. The tarnishing suggested it was real silver and the inscribed date of 1940 proved its age. Not an actual antique, but possibly of interest to a specialist collector. He put it to one side as he continued clearing the desk.

Karl found a file of typed sheets which looked like an old film script. It was for Casablanca and dated before the film was released, so might be of value to someone. Karl put it aside and picked up an old scrapbook. It contained some dusty looking pressed flowers and a tatty bit of yellowed paper covered in almost unreadable writing, some of which looked like latin. There were a few signatures, presumably celebrity autographs, and lots of pictures. The first was of Winston Churchill smoking one of his trademark cigars.

Quite a coincidence after discovering the cigar cutter. Next was another picture of Sir Winston, this time clipping the end off his cigar. Karl didn't recognise the gentleman on the next page. He recognised the following photo though. Karl was almost positive it was of Granddad's cigar cutter. It showed the little silver gadget as shiny and new, resting on a handwritten note. It said 'Good luck, Winnie' and was dated 1940. That was the date engraved on the cigar cutter and as far as Karl could remember also the date Sir Winston Churchill was elected as Prime Minister of England. Together they must be worth a fortune!

Karl flicked back to the autographs, in case one could possibly be Churchill's. He didn't find that, but he did find Ingrid Bergman's.

"Petunia!" he yelled.

She came running. "Yes, Dad?"

"Those ballet shoes... any particular colour you want 'em?"

Karl sold the cigar cutter along with the photographs and a letter from a fellow politician offering the great man the gift and therefore proving its provenance. The sale brought in enough money for Petunia's ballet shoes, and lessons for the following year. They booked a family holiday and replaced Karl's very battered car.

Soon the cash was gone. Karl went to look for the filmscript. After he'd spent some time working away in the attic he saw it had notes in the margins. By comparing the writing to her autograph, Karl decided they were made by Ingrid Bergman herself as notes of how she'd play her role. The script brought in enough to keep them in luxury for quite a while.

Karl again returned to the attic and removed a feather

from Cedric the stuffed swan. With the aid of a knife he 'discovered' the quill pen used by Linnaeus as he started work on his famous system for naming plants and animals. The quill, Linnaeus's notes and plant samples should raise enough money for Karl to start up his own antique business and for Petunia to have ballet shoes in every colour of the rainbow.

15. Honestly, Mother!

I don't steal things. At least not on purpose. Despite being a few years past retirement age, I'm not senile either. I want to get that straight from the start, just in case you've been talking to my daughter. Shelley's opinion of me just lately is a lot lower than it is of a certain other person, I'm sorry to say. Still, moaning never gets anyone anywhere, does it?

Sometimes I get the tiniest bit distracted, I will admit, but I'm perfectly safe out on my own; neither a one woman crime wave, nor a danger to traffic. Right, now that we're on the same wavelength, I'll tell you about the shoes. They're in a box on the passenger seat of my car and I didn't buy them. Men's, size eleven, brand new and decidedly expensive looking. I'm fairly certain they weren't there when I parked a couple of hours previously. I always put my handbag there and I'd have noticed them. Surely I would?

When they got there isn't the issue. Neither is how. What matters is getting rid of them. Shelley is meeting me here at twelve and I can't let her see them. The easiest thing would be to put them in the boot, but then what? If Shelley spots them a week from now, and discovers I've been driving around with a large pair of men's shoes that I just happened to find... Well, she might really feel she has grounds to doubt my honesty and mental processes. Mind you, she already claims to think that.

The library book incident last week is easily explained. The sort of simple mistake which until quite recently

Shelley would have considered amusing, rather than a weapon to use against me. I'd made my choices and put them on those scanning things they have now, instead of a librarian with a date stamp. As I was leaving I bumped into a friend who was returning a new John Grisham.

"I know you like a bit of crime," Margaret said and handed it to me.

We laughed over that and I put it with the others I was borrowing. Then we got chatting, as you do. By the time we said goodbye, I'd forgotten there was one book in my bag which I hadn't shown to the scanning machine.

The nice lady, who came to see why the alarm had triggered, completely understood. Most people are very understanding about such little mistakes. Margaret certainly is. The reason we laughed about my liking for crime is that I stole her cat. Sort of anyway and entirely unintentionally.

You've probably heard of the exact same thing happening to other people. Scooby, as I now know he's called, darted into the house as I came back from running a few errands. He miaowed pitifully and guessing he was a hungry stray, I fed him a bit of cooked chicken which he wolfed down. After that he came in for his tea quite often. It wasn't until I bought him a collar that Margaret realised he was being fed elsewhere. She attached a note to the collar and we've been friends ever since. Shelley gently teased me over the incident at the time. I doubt she would now.

Where was I? Oh yes, the shoes. Now, what am I going to do with them? The way she is now, if Shelley sees them on the passenger seat, she'll probably say I ram-raided a shop and demand I give up driving and pass the car on to her. She's tried that before, but to my mind if she wants a car, she shouldn't have given up her own.

Perhaps I can find the shop the shoes were bought from and someone there can help me work out what happened? I'm not so distracted by the problem that I don't notice that two spaces away from mine there's another car of the same make and colour. Not that surprising as there's a local dealer and they're a cheap make. A possible solution to the mystery pops into my mind. Would the same key work on both cars? Or had I left mine unlocked... again?

I hurry back and check I've locked mine. There's no need to try the door of the other car; the baby seat in the front, child's booster seat in the back and toys everywhere tell me the owner hadn't mistaken my car for theirs.

Moving away from that other vehicle, I glance around in case Shelley is early for once and assumes I've got mixed up. No sign of her, however I'm reminded of 'the time you got lost in a car park' as Shelley refers to it. Hilarious she considers it. Let's see if you agree.

Usually, when I come into town I park in more or less the same spot. That time, I was giving Shelley a lift and she was running late. Because of the delay, this end of the car park was full and I had to park over the other side. When we came back I remembered that alright, but once in the car she started saying how it would be best if I gave up the house now it's too much for me. It isn't, but we'd been through this before and I tuned out her words. Well, I say hers... Let's not go there. Anyway, on autopilot I reversed out the space and turned left as usual; into a dead end.

"Honestly, Mother. What are you doing?" Shelley demanded. A few weeks before, she'd have found it mildly funny and we'd both have had a giggle over it. She laughed when it happened, but not in a particularly pleasant way.

"Taking you to your flat, as you asked me to," I told my

once loving daughter, and had the car turned round and facing the right direction in moments.

Solving the problem of the shoes might take longer than that, especially as I can't see a shop front which matches up with the name on the shoe box and there's only five minutes until twelve; the time Shelley said she'd have to be taken home so she could be ready... Well, she has a date, I suppose you'd call it.

I spot a charity shop and take the shoes in there. They're very pleased about the donation and the fact that I give them my details so they can claim extra tax back or whatever it is they do. I'm pleased with the visit too as I spot a lovely jumper in a gorgeous turquoise shade. It's my size, only £3 and looks as new as the shoes. Of course I can't resist.

"Are you absolutely sure about the shoes?" the assistant asks. "If you took them back to the shop, I'm sure you'd get your money back."

"I don't have the receipt," I tell her which of course is true. I don't actually say I never did as I don't want her thinking I may have stolen them. She looks more trusting than Shelley, but looks can be oh so deceptive, can't they?

I spot my dear daughter hurrying across the car park as I return to the car at quarter past twelve.

"Twelve o'clock I said, Mother."

"Did you, dear?" I ask. She had, but I hadn't agreed to it. I love her of course, but these days she tends to take for granted that I'll do whatever she wants. I hate to argue with her, so I smile sweetly. "I must have forgotten. You know what I'm like."

She sighs theatrically. "Yes, I do. Honestly, Mother, you are the limit! First you forget to lock the car and then you turn up late. I'm freezing."

There's quite a lot wrong with that. For one thing she was as late as me. For another I'd checked I'd locked the car, you saw me, didn't you? Most annoying though is her tone. You'd think I'd deliberately kept her waiting in the cold.

"Why didn't you get in?" I ask. I almost add, "Rather than wait for ages by an unlocked car?" but resist. Despite knowing the car was locked the question I do ask is valid. Although I'd resisted giving her the car, I had parted with the spare key 'just in case'. Perhaps it's mean of me, but I try opening the door before unlocking it.

"It's not open now!" she snaps. "I meant earlier on. I tried calling you, but you've forgotten your phone again, haven't you?"

"Certainly not." I retrieve it from my handbag and switch it on. Sure enough, it shows a missed call from Shelley.

"Why did you turn it off?" she demands.

"I had coffee with Margaret and didn't want to be disturbed."

"I've told you to keep it switched on, charged up, and with you at all times in case I need you for something."

"So you have, dear." I know the instruction by heart. I'm certain she does too. I don't like it one little bit and I think by now you'll realise that's precisely why it wasn't on; a wise precaution on my part, not a foolish error.

"I locked the car after I put Darren's shoes in, then called to remind you to be more careful."

"Darren?"

"My boyfriend, Mother!"

Ah yes. The good looking young man who constantly offers me unwanted financial advice and would marry my daughter 'if only we had a big enough house for the two of us'. He makes no secret that mine would be perfect. He's the person who's convinced Shelley that I'd be much better off in a home. I'm sure he's a confidence trickster. I made the mistake of saying so to Shelley while she was still in the first flush of her infatuation. Things have been frosty between us ever since. She tries to pretend there's no possibility that I'm right and I try not to think of him at all.

"Shoes, you said?" I ask Shelley.

"He's had some handmade especially and I picked them up for him today."

"Even though he has your car?" I don't bother asking who paid; I know Shelley will have.

"Well, yes, but… The shoes!"

"What shoes, dear?"

"The ones I put on your front seat. They've gone. Mother, this is a disaster! Weeks he's waited for them. He'll be furious."

"Oh." I'm wondering if I should take her over to the charity shop. They have my details and presumably Shelley has the receipt, so it should be easy enough to sort out.

"This could end our relationship!" Shelley wails.

Perhaps she's right; when she accidentally scorched the suit she was ironing for him he'd made it clear another mistake would not be tolerated. Behind Shelley, two spaces down, a car pulls out.

"Look," I say. "It's the same make and colour as mine. You don't think you could have put them in that one by mistake, do you?"

"No, of course not!"

I can see she's not entirely sure.

"It's a simple mistake, the sort of thing which could happen to anyone," I tell her.

"I don't think Darren will see it that way."

"He will if he loves you." Which means he won't understand at all. I do though, not about the shoes I don't mean, but about the way she's treated me lately. She was taken in by a charming manner and handsome face.

I can see Shelley thinking. She looks so sad, I guess she's starting to understand.

"Shelley love, sometimes we see what we want to see."

"You're not talking about the car, are you?"

I shake my head, then hold her as she cries.

"I've been an idiot," she sobs.

"No, you just made a mistake. Come on, love. Let's go home and I'll make you a nice cup of hot chocolate with marshmallows on. That'll cheer you up."

"But, Mum I don't live with you now, remember? And I don't drink hot chocolate because it makes me fat."

"No, I don't remember any such thing. Now get in the car and direct me home. You don't want me getting lost in the car park again, do you?"

"No I don't." She wipes away her tears. "Maybe I had better go home with you. Someone needs to check the house for stolen cats." She's doing her best to smile.

One day soon we'll laugh again. Perhaps at her mistake, more likely at one of mine, but we'll laugh together.

16. I Can Explain

The security guard looked at my passport, at me, then at my ticket. I knew what he'd ask and launched enthusiastically into my explanation. I loved saying it. It had allowed me to join the plane in England, surely it would allow me through passport control at my destination?

Halfway through, I saw he wasn't as charmed as everyone else I'd told. My face flushed, palms were sweaty, throat was dry.

He spoke again.

"I … I don't understand."

He gestured as though telling me to stay. I stayed; running through airport security in a foreign country, leaving behind my passport and ticket home, wouldn't be sensible.

Where was Ahmed? He visited the toilet ages ago. Thinking he'd lost me in the arrivals crush and gone ahead, I'd approached passport control and handed over my documents.

I must have looked guilty; I often do. If the alarm sounds as I leave a shop I panic and struggle to find the receipt. When people bump into me I'm the first to apologise.

We met, Ahmed and I, at a friend's barbecue. She dropped ice on a seat while sorting out my drink. Ahmed sat down then got up quickly.

"Sorry, that's my fault,' I said, then got flustered

explaining it was nothing worse than melted ice.

He'd smiled at my confused explanation. "Don't worry, I was feeling hot anyway. I'm Ahmed Hamid."

"Kirsty Thursday."

"My lucky day."

Mine too, I'd thought. It took me less than an hour to fall for his charm, sultry looks and wicked sense of humour.

The security man was soon back with a large companion who asked, in English, if the passport and other documentation were mine.

"Yes." I wanted to explain but couldn't get the words together.

"Step please this way just moment, madam?"

I knew I didn't have a choice.

Inside the small room were my suitcases on a table, three plastic chairs, a grim faced woman and little else. There wasn't even a window to allow a glimpse of the exotic country I was almost in.

"Take please seat."

The woman put on rubber gloves. She didn't look like she enjoyed her job. That wasn't comforting.

This wasn't how I'd expected the trip to go when Ahmed announced he had a surprise and showed me the tickets.

"They don't match the name on my passport."

"Of course not, but you can explain," he'd assured me.

"And we'd have to leave straight away! I haven't got time to pack."

"Don't worry, Kirsty. I've taken care of everything."

I believed him. Even when I expressed concern about the cost, and he said it was all taken care of, I didn't worry. I didn't know we had to earn our trip by dropping off a package. He didn't mention that until we were airborne.

"Don't worry, I've done this lots of times. It's easy."

I'd said I packed the bag myself. You have to don't you? I bet loads of husbands say that when really their wives did.

"You taking holiday vacation?" the big man asked.

"That's right." I wasn't sure if I should mention Ahmed.

"Where staying hotel?"

"I don't know." I got really flustered then. It must look suspicious to have no idea where you're staying, but I hadn't asked. I'd trusted Ahmed when he said everything was sorted out.

"You Missus Kirsty Thursday?" He waved the passport which didn't match the ticket in he had in the other hand.

"Yes, but I can explain."

I didn't get the chance to try. There was a tap on the door. A rapid conversation followed. It's normal for people to sound angry when you can't understand the language, isn't it?

"You together here Ahmed Hamid?"

I nodded. The big security guard gestured to the person in the doorway who let Ahmed in.

I didn't understand much of his explanation but recognised the name of his employer. Ahmed works as a courier for an electricals firm, transporting delicate pieces of equipment.

As the male officials looked again at my paperwork the female officer returned my belongings to the cases. Was that a good sign?

I heard my name mentioned and guessed Ahmed was

saying his boss booked this trip as combined job and wedding present. You see we'd got married just the day before. The tickets were in my married name but of course I'd not had time to change my passport.

"Missus Kirsty Hamid, congratulations wedding your new husband. Please enjoy beautiful our country. The delay I apologise to and can explain." He looked really embarrassed.

"There's no need," I assured him. We'd all had enough explanations for one day.

17. Fitting End

He's dumped and humiliated her. She's now a women scorned; showing her fury. He must die.

How?

Accident, murder, cancer, volcano? Nothing is beyond her control. She will watch him ugly with pain, humiliated, begging forgiveness.

Or maybe she won't. Perhaps he'll just vanish without trace. Will he be missed and mourned, or quickly forgotten as though he'd never existed? It doesn't matter – he won't be back.

When you're a soap actor, you must never, ever upset the script-writer.

18. Not Missing Barney

Pippa glanced out the kitchen window. Her brother-in-law wasn't just sitting on the decking waiting for her to bring him food and drink; Hugo was hammering at a section of decking she'd just replaced. It had been no trouble for Pippa to remove the partially rotten pieces and fairly easy to cut new ones to fit, but she'd not made a good job of fixing them in place.

She put the full tea pot on the tray which already held chicken salad sandwiches, a bowl of crisps, salt, pepper, mustard, napkins... Everything she thought he could possibly expect to follow her offer of 'a sandwich and cup of tea'. She placed the tray on the table in the shade of the parasol.

"This looks great," Hugo said.

"Sorry about the smell. I think next door must have one of those strange arums lilies."

"Ah, that explains it. I wondered if a cat had left you a dead mouse or something."

"Oh! There's no fruit. Would you like some? I've got apples and... "

"Sit down, Pippa. This is more than enough."

"It's too much? I'm sorry. With you coming straight from work, I thought you might be hungry."

He chewed and swallowed the big bite he'd taken from his sandwich. "Which I am. Thanks, Pippa, this is perfect."

She gave him an uncertain smile and poured their tea, being very careful not to splash anything onto the saucers. That was easier than on many occasions in the past, as she didn't have a sprained wrist to contend with, nor the need to prevent her sleeve riding up to expose bruises.

They ate and drank for a while, without speaking. Hugo's silence didn't seem angry or accusing. Even so, she felt she should say something.

"Thanks for seeing to that last piece of decking. I'm not good at anything practical."

"I wouldn't say that. You've done a really neat job with the patching. And you hadn't done too badly considering you were using hammer and nails. When professionals put down decking, they use screws, or a nail gun. That's much easier for anything like this."

"Ah. That makes me feel a bit better." It was reassuring to know he thought she'd done her best and wasn't to blame for it not being entirely successful.

"I remember that corner was showing its age, but didn't realise it had rotted through," Hugo said.

"It hadn't quite, but it fell apart when I lifted it up to bury Barney." She gave a nervous laugh, in an attempt to show she'd been joking. It was so hard to say her husband's name with any cheer in her voice.

Hugo gave a polite chuckle. "Not sure anyone would blame you. That brother of mine… Well, let's not talk about him. Are you coping OK, Pippa? Anything you need?"

"I'm fine, thank you. Thanks to those pills of yours I'm sleeping properly." Actually she'd not needed them; her sleepless nights vanished just when Barney had. Hugo had been so insistent she'd need something, taken the trouble to fetch those he'd been prescribed and instruct her on how to take them, that she felt obliged to show gratitude. "And now you've seen to the decking there isn't anything I can't manage, I don't think."

"Let me know if there is. Putting up shelves, mending gates, assembling furniture, you know I enjoy all that sort of thing."

"Thank you. More tea?"

"Please."

This time Pippa successfully accomplished the task without even the slightest tremble of nerves. Pleased with herself she sat back… and felt the teaspoon slither from her grasp. It clattered onto the decking. "Oh no!"

As she reached for the dropped spoon, she managed knock it down the gap between two boards. "It's gone! Oh, Hugo, I'm so sorry."

"It's alright, Pippa. It was just an accident. I'm not Barney; I'm not angry."

No, he wasn't. Hugo didn't bully her into submission. His tactic was to smother her with kindness. "It was one of your mother's spoons," she admitted. "I should have been more careful."

"Like I said, it was an accident."

"Yes, yes of course it was." She took a deep breath, telling herself it would be fine if she just stayed calm. "I've got one of those grabber things for picking up litter somewhere. I'll look for it later and try to get it out with that."

"I'll have a go if you like."

"No! I mean thank you, but there's no need."

"I don't mind, honestly."

"Finish your tea first." She chattered brightly as he ate, but Hugo didn't forget his wish to help, and sent her to fetch the grabber.

When she came back, Hugo looked shocked.

"What's wrong?" she asked.

"There are bones down there."

"You must be mistaken. It's probably just sticks."

"It's definitely bones."

"A crow has dropped something then, or maybe it's a drumstick from the barbecue we had last summer?"

"They're big bones, Pippa. Ribs, a skull, and what I think is a thigh."

"What are you going to do?" she whispered.

"Call the police."

It didn't take long for the first two officers to arrive. After a quick look, they called for colleagues to join them. Soon the quiet road outside Pippa's home was crammed with police cars, scenes of crime vans, assorted unmarked vehicles, and a collection of neighbours trying to see what was going on.

As the police photographed and measured, two police officers asked to talk to Hugo on his own. He hadn't looked at Pippa since making his discovery and didn't do anything to acknowledge her before he turned his back and walked away.

Pippa was questioned in her lounge. She gave no explanation for the presence of the bones, nor supplied her husband's current whereabouts.

"He's left me," she told them. "For another woman. Hugo will tell you."

"When was the last time you spoke to your husband, Mrs Bridges?"

"The day he left."

"And you've not tried to contact him since?"

What would have been the point? "No," she admitted. Pippa worried that sounded suspicious, but knew that if they checked her phone records they'd soon find out.

"And until then, were you on good terms with him?"

She shook her head. Her doctor wouldn't reveal anything about her injuries without consent, but others would talk. Neighbours would have heard Barney shouting at her. Friends were concerned about how timid she'd become and the number of bruises she collected. Hugo knew the truth – and that he'd not heard from Barney for weeks.

Pippa wasn't informed of her rights or asked if she'd like to call a lawyer, but as the interview continued, she felt it was only a matter of time. The police officers questioned her gently, kindly even, but she knew they were suspicious. How could she not? The sound of decking boards being prised free was proof of that.

The officer who'd been asking questions stopped mid sentence. Pippa swivelled round to see what had attracted her attention. It was a young man in overalls.

"You'll want to see this," he said.

They followed him out, to what had once been Pippa's garden deck. At first all she could see were the backs of men and planks stacked on her lawn. They must have ripped up the entire decking area. As people shuffled along to make room for the new arrivals, she saw what looked like an almost complete human skeleton.

The bones were discoloured in places, but for the most

part gleamed pure, brilliant white. Whiter surely than they'd be naturally? The shapes weren't quite right either. Too even, too smooth, too little detail. That and the way they were connected together showed this was a plastic skeleton. The kind often sold very cheaply as a hallowe'en decoration. Alongside it was the decomposing carcass of a small bird, which explained the whiff of rotting flesh. Poor little robin.

Hugo apologised for wasting everyone's time.

"You did right to call us, sir."

Everyone agreed with that, Pippa included.

The police apologised for the damage they'd caused.

"I can see you didn't have any choice," she said. She almost added that it was rotten anyway, but stopped. She'd either have to request compensation from them or put in an insurance claim; she wanted enough to pay for a decent replacement.

"Have you any idea how it got there?" an officer asked.

Although it must be obvious to them that someone had prised up a board and slid the skeleton into place, Pippa shook her head.

"My brother has a rather unkind sense of humour," Hugo said.

Pippa, flushing at the memory of jokes he'd directed at her, thought the officers who'd questioned her so kindly were probably glad they'd not taken a harder line.

It took a long time for the police to finish taking statements and clear everything away. Hugo stayed until last. Finally they all left and she was able to go to bed.

She didn't wake until almost nine hours later. A quick glance outside confirmed the previous evenings events had really happened – and that Hugo was back. He waved up at her window. Pippa washed and dressed without hurry, then went down to let him in.

"I'm so sorry, Pippa. I can't believe I thought, even for a moment, that you'd ..."

"It's OK, Hugo." What she really meant was that she wasn't surprised he'd immediately thought the worst of her and been so quick to call the police. Barney was his brother after all, and even though he knew how Pippa had been treated, Hugo had never tackled him about it, nor withdrawn his affection for the man.

"No, it isn't. I know you better than that and it should have been obvious that it wasn't Barney down there. It's odd I've not heard from him for a while, but he was absolutely fine a couple of weeks ago."

"So, why call the police?" Pippa asked.

"It seemed so unlikely he'd really leave you. You're lovely and so good to him... and... I know he's not always like that to you."

That was an understatement.

Barney had been a real charmer once. Charming enough that she could understand why other women still fell for him. In her case they'd had almost a year of real happiness until things started to go wrong for him.

He had trouble with work, a health scare and then someone deliberately braked in front of his car in an attempted insurance scam. He'd got angry. Understandably so, but it wasn't fair he took it all out on her. Over the years, he sometimes seemed to shake it off, then another little problem would would occur. He'd bully her, or worse, then hate himself and punish Pippa for making him feel that way.

He'd had several affairs too. It had taken her far too long to realise none of it was her fault and it was never going to get better. So long that by then, he'd left of his own accord.

Hugo, prompted she supposed, from his feelings of guilt about having called the police when he suspected her of getting revenge on his brother, and of not helping her avoid Barney's anger, continued to apologise.

"Stop it, Hugo. You can't fix the past."

"No, but I can help you now. Let me replace your decking."

"That's kind of you." She supposed it was, but given his love of DIY projects it wouldn't be a big hardship. She wasn't going to let him push her into it though. Years she'd put up with that dreary grey wood, which got slippery in winter and splintered in summer. "After all this, I'm not sure I want more decking. Would it be very difficult to put in a patio?"

Hugo went out to have a look. Pippa followed.

"It would have to either be raised up like the decking was, or I'd need to put in some drainage. Other than that I can't see any problems."

"What kind of drainage?" She didn't want plastic pipes.

"A soak-away. Basically a really big hole filled with gravel."

"That sounds like hard work."

"I wouldn't mind."

"If you're sure? If it was raised up, I'd imagine something being underneath…" She shuddered.

"Great, that's settled then. I'll measure up and get some samples of paving for you to choose from."

"I want natural stone. Not small squares and not grey. Large rectangles in a warm honey shade."

"Oh. Right."

"Thanks, Hugo. Cup of tea?"

"Please."

Over the next few days Hugo drew up a list of what they'd need to buy, both for constructing the patio and so Pippa could keep him well fed with his favourite meals. He also discovered why he hadn't heard from Barney. He'd rowed with the new girlfriend, who'd threatened to call the police. Barney had taken her away on a holiday booked the same day in the hope of shutting her up. He'd been mugged on arrival, losing his phone and cash. Pippa felt a pang of sympathy for the other woman. Being trapped with Barney in a foreign hotel, when he was in the kind of mood which would result from such bad luck, was an awful thought.

Hugo hadn't exaggerated about the soak-away being a really big hole.

"I should put something up to make sure nobody falls in," he said once it was a couple of feet deep.

"How about putting the patio tables and chairs around it? Would that do?"

"I reckon so. They're quite sturdy."

He'd worked from the moment he finished at his office, until the light began to fade, stopping only to gulp down the supper Pippa prepared for him. He'd just left when there was a knock on her door.

"Have you forgotten something?" Pippa said as she opened the door. Instead of Hugo, her husband was there.

"Why the hell did you change the lock?" He seemed half puzzled, half furious.

She didn't blame him for being confused. Three times he'd left her and for the previous two he'd come back all too soon and continued as though nothing had happened. "You moved out, Barney."

"Well, I'm back."

Perhaps he was, but he had no bag and his car wasn't on the driveway. It was as though he wasn't sure of his welcome and was keeping his options open. She noted the bruises on his knuckles and scratch on his cheek. The new woman had stood up to him just as Pippa should have. Just as she must do now.

Pippa tried to block his way, but that angered him and he shoved past her. She didn't have much chance against him on her own inside the house, so ran through into the garden. It was dark; she'd switched the security light on permanently when Hugo was working in the dusk and afterwards must have turned it off, rather than back to motion sensor mode.

Unfortunately the lack of light didn't send Barney crashing into the drainage hole. He didn't seem to notice anything was different and just stood there yelling at her. Pippa wondered how easy it would be to whack him over the head with the shovel his brother had been using, push him in the soak-away and fill it with the gravel.

Tempted though she was, Pippa resisted the impulse. She wasn't an idiot and Barney was a lot bigger and stronger than her.

"You've really come back to me?" she asked.

"Haven't you been listening you stupid little… "

Pippa tried to close her ears until he ran out of insults.

"Would you like a beer?" she asked, as sweetly as she

could.

Clearly fooled by her act, he smiled. "And make us something to eat, will you?"

"Of course. Sit yourself down, I won't be a minute."

When she returned with his drink and snack on a tray, he hadn't leaned back on his chair and toppled into the hole as she'd hoped. She wasn't really surprised by that, nor even his grunt of thanks for the food. He probably thought all he needed was to flash her a smile, say a few polite words and she'd be back where he wanted her. Who could blame him? It had worked before.

"Cheese and pickle sandwich?" she asked, offering him the plate.

"Yeah, OK." Barney gulped down his food and drink, much as Hugo had the last few days. In some ways the brothers were very alike. She fetched him another beer.

"I'm tired," Barney said.

"I'm not surprised, love," she soothed. "I heard about your awful trip abroad and how things have been going wrong for you." That, along with the six sleeping tablets she'd mashed into the pickle, should soon knock him out.

"It's not fair," he slurred.

"Actually, I rather think it is." Pippa pushed on the back of his chair, hoping to pitch him into the drainage hole.

Barney, presumably realising something was up, tried to stand. He took a couple of staggering steps and did the job for her.

Then Pippa pulled on her gardening gloves, picked up the shovel and whacked him over the head. That was the one part of the entire job she'd not planned, but the hole wasn't very wide and Barney was wedged, so it needed a little bit of force to get him to the bottom. Pippa didn't mind and actually gave him a few more whacks than were strictly necessary, before shovelling in enough gravel to cover him completely.

She would tell Hugo she'd felt bad about him doing all the work and helped out. She thought he'd believe her, but it didn't matter too much. If he got suspicious again and called the police, well it was he who'd been seen to dig the hole, his fingerprints were on the shovel and his sleeping pills in Barney's body.

Once she'd finished, Pippa placed a rose on the tiny grave she'd dug for the robin. She hadn't killed the poor little thing; next door's cat had done that and left it for her as a present. For once she'd been grateful for his grisly offering, as the smell of fairly recent death had added the finishing touch to her plan.

19. Thieving Magpies

Lewis was keeping watch from his bedroom window. Usually he looked down into his garden, or across the fields to the small patch of woodland, so he could enjoy the sight of wild birds, rabbits and foxes. He was so lucky to have been able to retire to a cottage on the edge of a rural village where such creatures were plentiful. There was everything from tiny sparrows to the hawks which preyed on them, noisy, brazen pigeons to shy and secretive wrens. In the evenings he was treated to the magical beauty of starling murmurations. Sometimes he saw leaping deer in the far distance.

Recently Lewis occasionally trained his binoculars in the opposite direction. There'd been a spate of burglaries and there was just a chance he'd spot the culprit. He took care to avoid peering into house windows, but he did look into gardens and public spaces. That allowed him to enjoy colour from goldfinches, robins and blue tits, song from blackbirds and larks.

Whilst scanning the street he saw his neighbour, Oscar, striding up the path towards Lewis's house. He braced himself for another confrontation. The younger man was, in Lewis's opinion, a bully. He was taller, broader and louder than Lewis, very sure of himself and extremely unsympathetic with regards the natural world.

Lewis understood not everyone was passionate about wildlife, but most people were at least tolerant of the birds and other creatures which inhabited the neighbourhood. Lewis knew some of his neighbours were irritated when he suggested reducing the amount of plastic waste they generated, saying that wasn't practical with a family to feed. Others felt they didn't have time to crush dog food tins and yoghurt pots before recycling so hedgehogs didn't get trapped after crawling inside in search of food. However there were more who promised to keep these things in mind.

Some of Lewis's neighbours had revealed themselves to be real supporters of wildlife. Like him they grew nectar rich flowers, fed birds, put out water. A few had nesting boxes or bat boxes and enjoyed watching wildlife in their gardens.

Not long ago Lewis had seen Oscar trimming his front hedge which contained a blue tit nest and had asked him to leave the job for a couple of weeks.

"The chicks will have fledged by then. If you don't the nest will be vulnerable to predators or perhaps even abandoned by the parents."

Oscar had said, extremely rudely, that he'd do as he liked and continued using his electric trimmers. Lewis had kept his distance since then. He'd not wanted to see the likely fate of those chicks and doubted he'd be able to speak civilly to the man.

Knowing Oscar had called to see him, Lewis reluctantly made his way downstairs and along the hallway. He took a deep breath and pulled open his front door. There was no angry Oscar waiting impatiently on the step. Lewis didn't think he'd taken so long the other man would have given up, and although he'd not heard anyone knock, knew he'd not been mistaken in seeing him. Lewis's eyesight was still sharp. He stepped outside and spotted Oscar peering in through a window.

"Was there something you wanted?" Lewis asked.

"There you are!" Oscar said, as though Lewis had been deliberately hiding from him. "I've come about the thieving magpies."

"Oh?" The chattering, noisy creatures had a reputation for flying away with shiny trinkets, but Lewis felt sure it was rarely justified. With their smart black and white plumage, and the way they seemed always to be on watch, they were more like airborne police officers than avian villains.

"I know we've had our differences in the past," Oscar said, "but you are a neighbour, so I thought it only right to warn you."

"Oh?"

"Quite a few people locally have lost valuables to these birds. With so many coming into your garden you need to be careful. Warn your softhearted friends too. Almost everyone, except me, who's lost something is a nature lover."

Oscar claimed to have lost a precious watch to a feathered thief.

"What makes you think it was a magpie which took it?" Lewis asked.

"It was on my bedside table. There was no sign of a break-in and nothing else was taken, even though there are other things in the house which would have been as easy to take, are worth more and would be easier to sell on."

Admittedly that didn't sound like a normal burglar had been in and taken it, but it didn't automatically follow that a magpie was responsible. Perhaps the thief was taking things to order? From what he'd heard everything else taken was fairly small, and a particularly valuable example of whatever object it was.

"Thanks for letting me know." Lewis didn't mention that the burglaries were already common knowledge, and that Oscar must have known about them the last time they'd spoken.

From what Oscar said it did sound possible a magpie was responsible. Many birds were creatures of habit. Once they discovered a well-stocked bird table they'd return day after day. If a magpie had become brave enough to fly into houses and steal something then it would probably keep doing it. Even so Lewis wasn't convinced. Why would a bird have been attracted into the house? And could it really have carried away something so heavy?

Maybe that's because it was Oscar who'd told him? Two days ago he'd said another neighbour's smashed window was the result of bird strike. That was just about possible, but if a bird crashed through a window surely it would been killed, or inside stunned or panicking? Lewis didn't believe the bird could have simply flown away again unhurt. He was unsure why Oscar had been in a position to witness the incident, but why he'd lie about it was less of a mystery. Oscar always seemed to blame birds or other wildlife for anything which went wrong.

Not long ago he'd tried to bully Lewis into paying to replace the rickety fence between their gardens.

"Sorry, that one is you responsibility," Lewis had said. Oscar, who had a job in the council's planning department surely knew that.

"It belongs to me, but you're responsible for the damage. Foxes have been jumping over to get the bird food you put out and they've knocked it down."

That was just lies. Oscar knew no foxes ever jumped it – he had motion sensor cameras in the garden to see all his nocturnal visitors. The foxes came in through the hedge on the other side.

When Lewis refused to pay, Oscar had threatened legal action. Just like his threat to contact the environmental health agency about the rats he claimed were encouraged by the food Lewis left for hedgehogs and his feathered friends, that had so far come to nothing. Until then, Oscars's actions had seemed a personal vendetta against Lewis, but maybe there was more to it than that? Oscar seemed to be attempting to turn other people against wildlife too. Could the council be planning something controversial? Maybe they wanted to build on yet another green space, create a new road, put the local stream underground in pipes or do something else damaging to wildlife, and this was Oscar's attempt to reduce local objection.

Lewis's watch over the local wildlife became more vigilant. He paid special attention to the magpie nests. It was possible a bird had stolen things and, if they had, Lewis hoped to find out first and do something to avoid public opinion turning against the flying felon. In his younger days he'd have climbed up and retrieved the loot. It wouldn't be sensible to do so now, but maybe he could persuade a sympathetic individual to do it. There was a lad three doors down who might make a good accomplice. He seemed the sort not to mind taking a bit of a risk and he often looked into those local gardens which had birdtables.

Generally getting other local people more enthused by nature might help thwart whatever scheme Oscar was planning. That thought gave Lewis extra motivation for spotting anything unusual. The sighting of a Hoopoe,

Golden Eagle or wild boar was extremely unlikely, but would generate enough excitement to secure the safety of their habitat. Updates on the best places to see interesting, if less rare species, might gain some local support.

Of course he slept and ate, but he took his meals upstairs to consume at his vantage point and whenever he had to get up in the night he took a look outside. Occasionally he was rewarded by the sight of badgers waddling along under cover of darkness.

Lewis wasn't entirely alone in his vigil – he shared his suspicions with those he knew were most interested in wildlife and received offers to help keep watch. One of these neighbours had called to share her findings when Oscar once again strode up Lewis's path.

"I've located the nest in which the thieving magpie has hidden the stolen valuables," he declared. "I'm going to climb up and get them back." By the time he'd knocked on all the doors in the street, he'd gathered quite an audience.

Lewis and his friendly neighbour didn't want to give Oscar the satisfaction of joining the group, but couldn't help being curious. From a distance they observed Oscar and his entourage head for the only clump of trees in the immediate area which Lewis wasn't able sto watch from his bedroom window. Fortunately they were able to find an alternative vantage point which, thanks to binoculars and a birding scope, gave them an excellent view – and what they saw was very interesting indeed!

Oscar's antics had attracted a great deal of attention. Once he'd climbed back down the tree, reporters from the local papers and TV station bombarded him with questions. Lewis arrived in time to realise those people were there at Oscar's invitation. He displayed his precious watch, crowed about his cleverness in working out what had happened and exaggerated his bravery in rescuing the stolen items.

Oscar praised the efforts of the local police to solve the burglaries with such enthusiasm that it sounded sarcastic. It was probably meant to.

"I know you can't arrest the bird, but at least you have the satisfaction of knowing the case is closed," he told the two detectives.

He'd almost run out of steam when he spotted Lewis. "Here's our resident wildlife expert. Perhaps he'd like to add a few words," he sneered.

"I do have a question," Lewis said. "Other than your own watch, what else have you retrieved?"

Oscar emptied a tumble of shiny items from his pocket. Those people who'd lost valuables crowded round, hoping to spot items of their own. They were mostly disappointed as, although glittering brightly, the haul was composed of worthless trinkets.

"There must be more than one magpie stealing things," Oscar insisted.

"No, there's just one thief," Lewis countered. "A human one. You!"

"You can't accuse people of something like that without proof," Oscar roared.

"Oh? You've done it with local wildlife... But you're right, that isn't fair." He approached the TV cameraman. "Do you have equipment to look at these memory cards from the motion sensor cameras in my garden and that of my friends?"

Some images were of a man, who could have been Oscar, in the garden of the house where the window had been smashed. They made clear no bird was responsible for either the damage or the pendant which was later discovered to be missing. What was probably the same man had also been captured digitally in two other gardens where the owners had been burgled.

Oscar seemed as though he'd enjoyed enough publicity and would like to leave, but the crowd gathered around the screen made that impossible.

"Could be anyone," he said.

That was debatable until Lewis handed over the image card from the camera attached to his birding scope. That showed an empty nest, photos of Oscar climbing up to it and more of him repeatedly reaching in and then putting his hand into his pocket. From the ground no doubt it looked as though he'd taken the items from the nest, but on screen it was clear he'd had them already.

"It was you who stole people's jewellery and other valuables," Lewis said. "You used the pretence of being a concerned neighbour to loiter round houses and break in if the coast was clear."

The cheers and congratulations for Oscar were replaced by murmurings of seeing him looking in through windows, or having let himself into gardens.

Lewis continued, "And you attempted to turn everyone against local wildlife so they'd believe your claims that magpies were responsible and not look for the real thief."

The cheers resumed when one of the detectives read Oscar his rights.

"Maybe you'll appreciate nature a bit more once you've been inside and done a bit of bird," Lewis couldn't resist saying.

20. Don't Make Me Angry

You, my no longer dear, my no longer loved, my no longer husband, you made me angry. Every time you used the phrase, 'at some point in time' my anger increased. I felt it growing like a physical presence, eating my heart.

If something needed fixing, "I must do that, at some point in time," you'd say.

If we had problems to discuss, "Yes, my love. We must talk, at some point in time."

When there were arrangements to make. "Don't fret, love. I'll sort it out, at some point in time."

I wished you'd drop dead – at some point in time.

When you called me six times a day at work that made me angry. Were you checking up on me? Jealous a part of my life didn't involve you? My mouth clenched as I tried to prevent the screams in my head being released into the office. I wished I had a tape recording of high frequency sounds that deafen the listener to play when you called. How could I without hearing it myself and what if an operator was listening in? No, I couldn't do that.

When you rang me so many times there was nothing left to say and we spent the evening in silence that made me angry. I wanted to wrap the telephone cord around your neck and slowly tighten it until your fingernails were blue and you could dial no more. You're stronger than me. So I didn't try that.

When you always called, "Hello, it's only me," as you came through the door, that made me angry. Who else would it be? It was always you. Only you. You'd bored away all our friends. Speechless with anger that's the phrase isn't it? Anything I wanted to say would just have caused another argument, so I remained silent.

Then receiving no reply you called out again, "Hello, it's only me."

I wanted to balance a weight above the door to crush your head as you entered. You're tall; I wouldn't have got anything high enough. So I didn't try that.

When you insisted on taking me out to dinner, two days into each and every new diet, that made me angry. We always went to your favourite restaurant and you always had several drinks on arrival ensuring I'd be the one to drive home.

You always ordered far too much. When I was unable to eat it all you'd say, "I'm sorry. I thought you'd like it. I only did it because I love you."

You repeated variations of this phrase until I'd eaten everything, knowing consuming so much would make me feel ill all night. I would gladly have run you over in the car park. Felt the lurch as the high bumper made contact with your fat body. You're a big man and I wasn't sure there was space to get up enough speed to knock you down. If all I managed were to bump into you I'd have to listen to yet another lecture on my lack of driving ability. Listen to it repeated endlessly. To my friends, the neighbours, your mother, my mother, anyone who'd listen. Sometimes even to people who clearly weren't listening. These same people suffered through your scathing remarks on my DIY skills too.

If they'd known how many months ago I'd been informed that putting a plug on was, "Nothing you need worry about, love. I'll do it, at some point in time."

If they'd known for how many months I washed your shirts by hand in the sink next to the brand new washing machine they may have understood my having a go myself. Most would have felt some sympathy for me even if I did leave a loose live wire. Yes, I nearly tried that.

When you bought me tacky gifts, I didn't want and we couldn't afford, that made me angry. Blood surged through my mind making concentration difficult as I tried to talk to you about my financial worries.

"Yes, love, we must sort it out, at some point in time," you'd pretend to agree.

I tried explaining that when I'd said I wanted you to show me you loved me I meant with affection not something in a plastic bag. A friendly word or hug would have been far more acceptable than an increase on the credit card bill. We argued then and I wanted to take the carrier bag and hold it over your head until your breath no longer sucked the plastic in and out. It seemed ungrateful; you'd been trying to do the right thing.

"I thought you'd like it. I only did it because I love you," you said yet again.

When you bought me a nasty ornament to apologise I realised you'd never understand. It wasn't anger then that made me smash the horrible thing with a claw hammer. It was cold, calculating fury. I had every intention of adding the slivers to your lunch for you to fork quickly into your greedy mouth.

I couldn't do it. If you survived I'd have had to nurse you. You were never an uncomplaining patient; your whining would have been annoying. No, I couldn't risk that.

I was considering an alternative plan as you came through the front door.

"Hello, it's only me."

I kept calm as you asked me to help with the minimum payment on the growing credit card bill. I quietly pointed out that without the unnecessary gifts this bill would be lower, not higher than the previous one.

"It's only because I love you that I like to buy you things."

I knew that, in your way, you did love me. I knew too that you'd always annoy me.

Well, that 'point in time' when we could have sorted out our problems has come and gone. Maybe I did love you once but no longer.

Now it really is only you and I'm your wife no more.

21. 'Must Read' Books

Heather sank gratefully onto a seat on the train. Thank goodness she'd reserved one! The way her day was going, if she hadn't, this fairly empty train would have been full of football supporters, Girl Guides on a day out or another unexpected large group of people.

She ran her hands through her hair, in an attempt to fluff it up, and dabbed her mouth with lipstick. It probably didn't make her any more attractive, but she felt she should make some sort of effort for the start of her holiday. On the seat opposite was a discarded newspaper. Unfortunately, it was the same as the one she'd read at lunchtime. Heather would have to find something else to occupy her for the journey.

Her plan had been to buy herself a good book and some naughty sweet treats before catching the train. It was a plan which was never put into practice. The day hadn't gone well, from when she realised she didn't have enough milk for her breakfast, right up until her boss had kept her late at work.

The milk was her own fault; because she was going away, she hadn't thought it worth buying another pint. None of the other problems were of her making though. Her weekend bag was placed in an out of the way corner, yet still someone had managed to spill a mug of coffee over it. She'd spent the lunch break cleaning it and checking her clothes were all dry. Then her boss had flown into a panic at the thought of her being absent for a week and attempted to give her a fortnight's work to complete before she left. It wasn't fair; because of poor health she'd recently reduced her hours and therefore her salary, but her boss didn't seem to realise that meant he should reduce her workload.

Still, she hadn't missed the train and she didn't have to stand. Heather resolved not to let a few little setbacks ruin her break. So what if she didn't have anything to read and was without the chocolates and frothy coffee she'd promised herself. She could survive a train journey, even one all the way to Scotland, without them and there would probably be a buffet service.

It was a shame it was already getting dark, she could have enjoyed the scenery and glimpses into gardens otherwise. Instead, she had to content herself with a spot of people watching. There was a young couple opposite, chattering away in French. Heather could only understand a very few words and amused herself guessing what their conversation was about. Planning the next stage of their foreign adventure, perhaps? They sat close and often touched each other's arm or hand, so were probably boy and girlfriend rather than siblings. The way they giggled together and seemed to finish what the other was saying, suggested this wouldn't be their last holiday together.

The only other person she could see, without it being obvious she was watching, was a man of about her own age. Maybe a little younger, she decided. His hair, although sprinkled with grey, was thick and hardly receding at all. He had a pleasant face, especially when he smiled. He smiled a lot, frequently bursting into laughter, as he read a book.

Heather had just decided the man was quite attractive when his mobile rang. They were in one of the 'quiet' carriages, yet he answered the call and spoke loudly and at length. Ordinarily she liked the sound of a Scots accent, but the volume and fact he shouldn't have been on the phone at all meant she didn't enjoy listening to him.

She was dismayed when he said, "I'm on the train to Edinburgh. Should get in just after ten." Then he pulled a can of beer from his bag and started drinking.

The French couple got off at the next station. Nobody else joined Heather's carriage. Great, Heather had hours on the train, with only a rude, and possibly drunk, companion.

The man returned his attention to his book and started laughing again. Heather tried to see what it was called so she could get a copy herself. She could do with a laugh. She'd just decided to look for an empty seat somewhere else when she saw the man's head was nodding. Soon he was snoring. Heather reached over and removed the book from his slack grip.

Heather moved into another compartment and chose a seat in the corner where she wouldn't be so easily spotted. It wasn't a marked quiet carriage, but the other occupants were either reading papers or dozing. That made the laughing man's actions seem all the more inconsiderate. Who was she to talk? She'd just stolen a book! No, borrowed one, she told herself. They'd both be on the train for hours, she could give it back later.

She couldn't quite convince herself of her innocence though. If she hadn't been feeling guilty, why had she walked with the book hidden in her coat and fumbled to turn a couple of pages, hoping she had it the right way up, so it would look as though she'd already started reading it, not just 'acquired' it. Heather was in luck. She'd held the book the right way and so had successfully skipped the intro and dedications and got straight to the start of the story.

Soon it was her annoying everyone with her snorts of laughter. The book really was excellent. Too good. She didn't realise how long she'd been reading until she needed the toilet. When she went in search of one, she saw she'd almost reached her destination. In a panic, she went looking for the man, whose book it was, trying to think of a tactful way to return it.

The man wasn't in his seat. Heather used the toilet, then continued reading the book until she reached Edinburgh. In her hotel she felt guilty. She hadn't really tried very hard to find the man and she knew why. The book was so good she had to finish it. He'd be upset he'd lost it though. She must return it if she could.

Heather looked at the front, hoping there might be a name. Better than that, there was a library lending record sheet. It appeared to be a privately owned library. She'd never heard of it, but there was an address. Thank goodness, she could return it and he'd be able to borrow it again. Best of all she could read the rest without feeling guilty.

She calculated how many pages were left and rationed herself to just a sixth of them each day. Heather enjoyed visiting the museums and galleries in Edinburgh, took pleasant walks along the streets of the old town and a spent hours window shopping and present buying in the dozens of shops in Ocean Terminal shopping centre. Whenever she felt tired, there was always a café, tea shop or restaurant serving wonderful food and drinks. She didn't get tired as often as she'd feared she might.

Her short holiday was doing her good and she felt stronger than she had for months. Walking the Royal Mile became more than just a dream and she easily managed the climb up Arthur's seat, with just a couple of stops to admire the view and catch her breath. The highlight of each day though, was to curl up on the bed in her room with a box of chocolates, coffee laced with whisky from the mini-bar and the book. She read as slowly as she could, savouring every sentence.

During the days, as she visited the tourist highlights, Heather remembered lines from the book and laughed all over again. When that happened during the open top bus tour, Heather found she wasn't crowded by other visitors for long.

On her last day, Heather returned the book. The library was hard to spot, in fact she'd walked past it earlier in the week without noticing it. The door, which opened straight onto the narrow street could have been that of a terraced house, but for the brass plaque bearing its name.

Inside, the library was small, but absolutely crammed with books. Every wall was lined with shelves and more shelves were squeezed into a claustrophobic maze throughout the downstairs rooms. A sign indicated there were more books to be found upstairs, by those brave enough, and small enough, to negotiate their way up the book piled steps.

None of the books looked as though they'd be available in the bookshop of her home town. That sold all the best-sellers and seven types of coffee, but the books there didn't have the appeal of the ones she was surrounded by in Edinburgh. Some looked as though they might be very old, some were huge with bright covers, some tiny and bound with leather. Heather wished she'd come in earlier as every book seemed to be begging her to read it.

Heather couldn't allow herself to browse the shelves or she risked missing the train home. After the briefest look round, she queued at the counter behind a woman returning a pile of books, which all seemed to be by the same author. She must have kept them for ages as she was asked to pay a wapping fine.

When it was Heather's turn, the assistant said, "There's a fine, I'm afraid."

"Yes, I'll pay that." It was her fault the book was late, so she didn't mind.

"Thirty-seven pounds."

She paid. What else could she do? The alternative was to say, "But I only stole it a week ago." Besides, although thirty-even pounds was a lot for a book, it wasn't too high a price for a week's entertainment.

Heather no longer felt guilty about taking the book from the man as it seemed she'd done him a favour by saving him the fine. As she left, she heard the person who'd been behind her in the queue nervously say, "I'm returning this for a friend. I hope it isn't late?"

"Sorry, it is actually. Will you be paying your friend's fine, or shall I contact him?"

"It's OK, I'll pay it."

Heather wondered how much it would be as she rushed to catch her train. Looking for the bookshop meant she again didn't have time to stop to buy something to read. She did just have time to get a coffee and chocolate muffin though and she easily found a seat.

When she'd finished her treat, Heather looked at the people around her. Opposite was a woman reading a paper. She folded the paper over, revealing a picture of someone Heather recognised. She tried not to stare.

"I've finished, would you like to read it?" the woman

offered.

"Thanks." Heather took the paper and studied the photo. It was of the man she'd stolen the book from, she was sure. The caption read, 'Entrepreneur owner of private library reports record profits!' She read the article. The secret to his success, he said, was that he only stocked books people couldn't resist.

Heather had another week of holiday owed the her. She planned to visit Edinburgh again and to register with the library she'd found. If she read fast and returned the books before she left, she wouldn't have a fine. Already though, she was wondering how easy it would be to post them back, if she borrowed more just before she left.

22. On The Run

Bert had hoped for a nice relaxing afternoon with his feet up, mug of tea to hand and snooker on the telly. Marjorie had other ideas. All his wife's ideas would have him on his feet, something other than a mug in his hands and the television off. It wasn't as though Bert had no choice in the matter; Marjorie had made that perfectly clear. She didn't mind if Bert mowed the grass or started painting the bathroom, just as long as he shifted himself from the sofa.

"A disgrace, that lawn. What the neighbours think, I can't imagine," she said as she dusted the already neat and tidy lounge.

Bert knew what the man from next door thought – that Bert was lucky not to be sent out every other day to ensure that no weed ever came close to spoiling the perfect sheet of grass that poor man's wife insisted on gazing at when she did the washing up.

"There's enough of the yellow paint left to give the bathroom walls a couple of coats," Marjorie said as she pulled the cushion out from behind him and plumped it. "I think that would really brighten the room up."

He had to admit she was right there. It would brighten up the bathroom to such an extent that the landing and bedrooms would look dull and tired in comparison. Marjorie would then want them painted or papered too. Then she'd want to go shopping for new curtains.

This was not how Bert had pictured his retirement.

Slouched unshaven on the sofa in a saggy cardigan watching the telly hadn't been what he'd imagined either. Surely there were still things he could do? Things that would get him out the house so that Marjorie could go back to watching the daytime soaps between stints of housework and wouldn't feel obliged to spend every waking minute dusting, vacuuming and polishing.

The phone rang. Bert didn't even think of trying to answer it; the call wouldn't be for him. He didn't try to listen to Marjorie's side of the conversation either as he doubted it would be at all interesting. Probably she'd inform the caller that their home already had windows, or a kitchen, or insurance and hang up. Then she'd tell him all about it whether he was interested or not.

Marjorie didn't hang up after thirty seconds, which was unusual. She also wasn't speaking, which was more than unusual. She did gasp a few times and her fingers seemed to be gripping the receiver much harder than was necessary.

"He can't have! … You don't think… ? Oh Cheryl, whatever are we going to do?"

That last bit got his attention. Something awful had happened to their daughter. He had to help her. He'd want to anyway of course, but this might be his chance to prove that retirement hadn't turned him into a cross between an inefficient handyman and an extra item to dust. Bert tried to gesture his intentions to Marjorie.

"I think your dad is offering to help."

Bert nodded vigourously.

"Don't worry, love," Marjorie assured their daughter. "Your dad will know what to do."

The confidence in her voice made him pull his shoulders

back and stand tall.

"It's Peter, " Marjorie informed him.

"What's happened to Peter?" Bert asked. Their son-in-law was a pleasant chap. A bit quiet maybe and away working for long stretches of time but a good husband to Cheryl.

"He's run away!"

"He can't have!"

"He has. She asked him about his last job and he went crazy and just walked out, so she said."

"You don't think… ?"

"I don't know what to think," Marjorie said.

"Poor Cheryl. What are we going to do?"

"Maybe you could find him, Bert. Talk to him man to man?"

Bert knew he had to try. He swapped his slippers for shoes, grabbed the car keys and roared off. He could only hope such decisive action had reassured Marjorie and that he'd soon think of somewhere to look. He decided to drive to Peter and Cheryl's home and see if an idea presented itself on the way.

As he passed the pub on the edge of the housing estate, Bert saw someone jump over the low wall outside and sprint across the car park. It was Peter. Bert reversed into the car park, leapt out and ran round the side of the pub. He called out to his son-in-law.

Peter spun round to face Bert. The younger man was red faced and sweaty and clutching a handful of cash.

"Bert! I can explain…" he said as he gasped for breath.

"You'd better had," Bert said.

Before Peter could try, a man came running along the

path. "Don't let him go, mate. He's a thief!"

Bert listened amazed as the man, who identified himself as the landlord, explained.

"Looked nervous he did. Should have known there was something wrong, but I'm a trusting sort. I served him and he gulped down half his pint, then ran into the gents. I thought his unease was because of his need to use the facilities. He didn't come out so I wondered if he was ill. When I came to look, I saw he'd escaped and you'd stopped him. Will you hold him while I call the police?"

Peter said, "I can explain."

The landlord didn't look convinced. Bert wasn't convinced either, but he knew he couldn't go home and tell Marjorie and Cheryl he'd helped have Peter arrested. If the landlord went to call the police, Bert would have to take Peter away and then there'd be two of them on the run.

"Let's hear what he's got to say for himself first," Bert suggested in a tone far more assertive than any he'd used since his retirement.

"I wasn't trying to get away without paying," Peter claimed. "I've got money."

As Peter waved the bank notes at the landlord, Bert remembered Peter had been running towards, not away from, the pub. He told the landlord that.

"I ordered the drink with every intention of paying, but suddenly realised I didn't have any cash on me. I've... I've had a bad day and couldn't bring myself to admit the truth, so I climbed out the window, ran down to the cash machine in town and then came back with the money."

The landlord appeared to be thinking.

"He's my son-in-law, I can vouch for him," Bert said.

The landlord looked from Peter to Bert. "Well, you certainly don't look like any kind of criminal gang. You have been running, I see that, and you did come back."

He turned away and walked back to the pub's entrance, leaving Peter to follow.

Peter paid for his drink, which was still on the counter and offered Bert one.

"Thanks, lad. Better make it a half as I'm driving. Talking of which, I'd better go and park the car properly and lock it."

When he returned, Bert suggested they move away from the bar. "You have some explaining to do."

"It really happened just as I said it did. Thanks for vouching for me though, some people would have taken one look at the mess I'd got myself into and wanted nothing to do with me."

"True enough, but I'm not some people; I'm your father-in-law. I think you'd better tell me what's going on."

Bert couldn't decide which of them was more surprised by his tone.

"Thing is that I've been working very hard lately. Cheryl was very supportive through it all. She never complained when I was home late or had to be away. She always had a meal waiting when I came home and clean clothes packed when I left."

"Just like Marjorie did with me," Bert said.

"Exactly. But now I've got some time off…"

"She's collecting paint charts and gardening catalogues and treating you somewhere between an inefficient handyman and an extra item to dust."

"Yes. I didn't want to end up like you; no offence. I

thought it would be better if I was out the house, so I came down here. I was hoping they'd have a telly with the snooker on."

Bert looked round, "No television, they've got a pool table though," he pointed out.

"Yes, bu …"

"You've got a mobile phone, haven't you?"

Peter handed it over.

Bert made his call. "I've found him, Marjorie… Yes, yes he's fine. Just a misunderstanding… Choosing wallpaper… Yes… That's what I thought. I'll bring some samples."

He handed the phone back. "You tell Cheryl the same, then we'll have time to play at least a couple of frames." Bert held up some wallpaper samples. "Marjorie picks these up whenever we go shopping, they've been in my wallet for weeks."

"We'll be decorating soon, then?"

"Of course not. They won't accept the first suggestion we make; they'll want to see lots more before deciding these were OK after all. Then I don't think we should start until we've chosen paints. Could take weeks, maybe months. I reckon that by the time you're back at work, Marjorie will have decided she prefers me coming here than being at home making a mess with paste and paint. If I occasionally cut the grass before I leave home, I think I'm going to enjoy a long and happy retirement."

23. Only Joking

Betty could feel a hot flush coming on. The meeting with the bank manager was quite embarrassing enough without that. David had changed the PIN and security details for all their bank cards and accounts and then promptly forgotten them. He claimed he'd done it as a joke, something the bank manager had initially found hard to believe, but which didn't surprise Betty one bit.

Now they had to prove who they were before they could pay their bills and employee's wages. The bank manager, after a few minutes of conversation with David wasn't having such a hard time believing he would have done such a thing, but couldn't understand why and clearly didn't see the funny side. Betty sympathised as she felt exactly the same.

"Wish I had some bread," David said. "I could make toast." He held the passports they'd brought as identification up to Betty's flaming cheeks and roared with laughter.

She was furious and the bank manager looked very uncomfortable. In a way though it was helpful as the bank manager was by then totally convinced that David was the sort of person who'd find it amusing to have his wife do the week's shopping and then be unable to pay, because he'd done something stupid.

As they walked out, David did have the grace to apologise, but only for forgetting the new numbers. He added, "I know what'll cheer you up."

"No you don't, David. You have absolutely no idea how humiliating this has been for me, nor how angry I am with you."

"Well sorry, I'm sure. I remember when you liked my jokes." He sulked all the way home which was a great improvement on his usual stupid chatter and pranks.

It was true – she had liked his jokes once. That was back when they were occasional and amusing. He just wasn't funny anymore. Actually it was worse than that. Many of his tricks were downright mean. Maybe he didn't really intend to be nasty, but he certainly put a moment of laughter for himself far above the long term upset of anybody else.

Last week he put salt in place of sugar in the storage jar, so it ended up in the custard she was making. Nobody noticed until it was poured over every slice of treacle tart. Ages it had taken to do all that fancy latticework on top and it was her father-in-law's favourite. He'd been so pleased she'd made it for him, right until he'd taken a bite. Now he felt responsible for the time and effort she'd wasted. David didn't seem to care at all that his father had felt bad about the situation.

It wasn't just Betty who suffered from David's misguided humour. He played 'jokes' on his staff. He locked one woman in the stationery cupboard last week.

"How was that funny?" she asked when he told her.

"Everyone else laughed."

"They have to, you're the boss."

"It's not that, it's just some people don't get a joke. Most of my staff do and they found it hilarious."

"Including the victim?"

"No sense of humour that girl. I was just trying to get her

to lighten up. Put some of them dried worms you feed to birds in her lunch. Should have seen the look on her face!"

"I hope you haven't caused her to relapse."

"What? She's not ill or something is she?"

She wasn't, but Betty didn't tell him straight away. Maybe the fright would make him think twice before he upset anyone else. It didn't work. When David found out he just clapped her on the back and said, "Good one, Bet! You really had me going there. I'm educating you at last."

Betty thought that if he liked that one he'd love her putting rat poison in his dinner. Unfortunately she didn't have any handy. She went round to her elderly neighbour.

"Lovely to see you, Betty dear. Do you have time for a cup of tea?"

"I'd better. If I don't keep away from David for a bit I'm going to do something I might regret."

"Ah! Come and sit down and I'll cut you a piece of cake and you can tell me all about it."

Florence was sympathetic as she'd been a victim more than once. David gave her little dog rubber toys in the shape of severed fingers or hand grenades. Last month he'd put something in her bin which played cries for help. Florence, thinking perhaps a small child was trapped, lifted the lid but saw only rubbish. She couldn't reach far enough inside and feared if she pushed the bin over she'd cause injury so yelled for help. Several neighbours, Betty and David included, came running.

No child, nor anything else to explain the cries had been found so of course it seemed Florence had imagined them. Betty learned the truth a few days later when she'd heard the same cries coming from the freezer. She'd reassured

Florence it wasn't she who was losing her grip on reality.

Betty reminded her neighbour of the incident. "I wish now one of us had called the police over it."

"You can't do that to your own husband."

"If someone doesn't do something soon he's going to hurt somebody."

"Perhaps if we gave him a taste of his own medicine he'd realise these pranks aren't so funny?"

"I'll see if I can think of something. Thanks, Florence. It's helped to talk anyway."

Later that evening Betty and David heard Florence going out with her dog. "Where shall we go tonight, my little Poppet?"

"What d'you think she'd do if it ever answered her?"

"Have a heart attack?" Betty said.

"Nah. Reckon she'd love it."

A few days later David staggered in, his face pale and clammy and he seemed to be having trouble breathing. "I've killed old Florence," he gasped.

"Hilarious," Betty said. "But you needn't think I'm going to help dig a hole to bury her."

"I'm not kidding, Bet." He sank into a chair. "It was supposed to be a joke. I put a phone under the bench she sits on most days. She asked the dog if he wanted a treat and I asked for cheese and onion crisps. Then she collapsed. I tried explaining over the phone but there's no sound and she's not moving."

"Call for help!" Betty pushed the phone towards him then raced over the road to the park. She could see Florence stretched out, perfectly still on the bench.

"Florence, it's me Betty. Hang on, help is coming."

Florence's eyelids fluttered. "What's that? Oh, Betty dear, what's happened?"

"David played one of his stupid tricks on you."

"Oh yes, I remember. I recognised his voice and decided to play a little trick of my own. I pretended to faint and then lay still. I must have fallen asleep. Did it work do you think?"

"Oh yes! It hasn't half given him a fright. I'd better go and stop him ringing the ambulance."

"I'll take Poppet home, then come round and perhaps between us we can persuade him to stop his silly pranks."

They didn't get the chance. David had managed to call the ambulance. It arrived just in time to revive him – the shock of apparently killing Florence and then running all the way home from the park had brought on a heart attack. If that didn't make him see sense over his unkind pranks then nothing would.

It seemed touch and go for a while, and while he was so vulnerable Betty had a glimpse of the more gentle David she'd married. She so hoped that man was back for good, but when Betty visited him on the third day although he was still wired up to a machine he was sat up in bed chuckling.

"What's so funny?"

"See that chap there? He had to give a urine sample and I managed to empty the ink from my pen into it. Can't wait to see what the docs make of that. Reckon they'll give him all kinds of tests."

"That'll be horrible for him."

"Funny though!"

"Worrying for his family."

"Why are you getting in a state over them? It's me you should be thinking of."

"Hmm. Well they didn't need to give poor Florence any tests." Betty hung her head so he wouldn't see her expression.

"Oh. Well, she was old and no fun."

"You killed a nice old lady and you don't care one bit!"

"I didn't mean for her to die."

"That's all you have to say?"

"No. I hope whoever moves into her place next is up for a joke."

"No need to wait," whispered an eerie voice.

The curtains around David's bed twitched and then Florence came into view.

"She's a ghost, come back to haunt me!" David shrieked.

"Noooo. Not to haunt, just to have a little joke. It might be funny if I pressed this switch, don't you think?"

As Florence stretched out a hand, a weird bubbling sound came from David. His body shook and his arms waved wildly, right up until the moment the monitor flatlined.

"Oh dear," Florence said. "Perhaps he wasn't laughing after all."

Betty shrugged. "No sense of humour that man. That's his trouble."

25. I Want To Be Alone

On the morning of Dinah's wedding, she woke early. The dawn chorus was especially loud as the birds were eagerly trying to attract their mates, but that wasn't what had woken her. Neither had she been roused by any doubts about marrying Austin. No, it most definitely wasn't that. It was just that ever since childhood she'd been an early riser. Back then, first thing in the morning was the only time she got any peace, as her sisters never got out of bed until they had to. Dinah had maintained the habit, and still enjoyed the quiet of the early mornings.

That's partly why she'd spent the night before her wedding alone in her flat instead of at her mum's place. Mum and Dinah's sisters had wanted her to stay there overnight, but she'd declined.

"I'll disturb everyone else when I get up," she'd pointed out.

"You could have a lie in, love."

"I won't be able to sleep later than usual, and if I lie awake I'll just start fretting," she told them.

Either of those scenarios, the fretting alone or disturbing the others, would have put her on edge, but weren't her main reason for not being with her family right then. It wasn't that Dinah didn't love her mum and sisters – she did very much. The trouble was her need to be alone sometimes. That had caused numerous problems in the past, putting strain on friendships and even broken up a previous engagement.

Dinah's family usually understood she was different from them and their love of constant company and chatter, but sometimes forgot to give her space, and occasionally struggled not to take it personally when she needed a break from them. Dinah simply hadn't wanted to risk any upset feelings on her wedding day. Not for any of them. She really was looking forward to seeing them all later. Everyone would fuss around her and it would be chaotic fun. She just needed her peace and quiet first, so she'd be calm enough to enjoy her big day.

Had she made a mistake? Not with the marriage, she really wasn't worried about that, but by having so much time alone beforehand. There was nearly two hours before the taxi was due to pick her up and take her to her childhood home. There was nothing for Dinah to get ready – it was all at Mum's. She'd had breakfast, cleared up, was already showered and dressed. Much as she needed time alone, such a long period with nothing to do probably wasn't such a good idea. Just as would have happened if she'd lain awake that morning, she would start to go over and over things in her mind. Time to think was a good thing if you needed to work something out, but could be a problem when you were already sure.

Ideally she'd have gone for a good long walk on the beach, but couldn't risk driving herself there. She didn't think she was likely to suddenly give way to nerves, but was excited enough about marrying Austin that she might not give the road her full attention. Even more likely were traffic delays or trouble parking which would ruin her calm. And she couldn't ask anyone else to drive her down and then expect them to sit and wait while she walked alone. Austin would have done it and understood perfectly, but she was keeping to the tradition of not seeing or hearing from him before the ceremony.

Just after seven, her phone beeped to say she had a text. The screen showed it was from the taxi company. As they were ferrying guests to the wedding, Dinah to her mum's, and the happy couple to their hotel that night and the airport tomorrow, she'd stored the number in her contacts.

The text read, 'If you're ready now, there's time for you to walk along the beach before going to your Mum. Can drop you off and pick up as required. If you don't want to, or don't reply, you'll be picked up at 9 as previously arranged.'

Perfect!

Austin must have organised that for her. Not only did he understand her need to be alone at times, he was so good at knowing when a few moments peace would calm her that she never did feel the need to get away from him. Maybe that phrase about the right person being your other half was true?

She texted back. 'Please pick me up as soon as possible'.

Dinah ran out and jumped into the back of the taxi the moment it arrived. As they pulled away, she asked, "Have you been told where to drop me off?"

"I know where to take you, Dinah."

No! It couldn't be... could it? She leant forward to check the driver wasn't who he sounded like.

On no – it really was Robert! The man she'd nearly married until she realised that would mean she'd never be alone. Like her family, he didn't share her occasional need for that. Unlike them he'd never accepted it. When she tried to explain she wasn't comfortable sharing every available moment and every thought with him, he'd been hurt. Dinah had known that either he'd continue to feel that way, or she'd feel trapped and smothered, so had ended their engagement. He hadn't taken it well and bombarded her with calls and flowers and constantly tried to see her. She'd had to threaten to report him as a stalker to the police before he stopped.

"What are you doing here, Robert? Kidnapping me?" she demanded.

"No, although at one time I thought of that. Then, when you mentioned the police, I realised just how crazy I'd been. I'd been so scared of losing you, I wouldn't let you out of my sight – and that's just why I did lose you, isn't it?"

"Yes."

"See, I've learned my lesson."

"And stolen a taxi and come to try and win me back?" She instantly regretted snapping. It was probably best to hide her panic until he had to stop for a red light or something, and then make a run for it. If he didn't guess what she was planning, maybe she could get away from him.

"No! I really am a taxi driver. I saw your family's bookings for today. I admit that when I realised you were getting married I was jealous and intended to try to persuade you to give me another chance."

"But you realised that would be a mistake?" She spoke gently, hoping he really did realise.

"Not until I saw you with Austin. You looked so happy. Happier than you'd looked when we'd been planning our wedding. I knew then that you were right and it would never have worked out between us."

"OK… so what are you doing here now?"

"Taking you to the beach."

"And letting me get out the car?"

"Yes, of course." He stopped the car and turned to look at her. "Oh God, Dinah, I'm sorry – you really did think I was kidnapping you?" His distress was obvious.

"Just for a moment."

"I'm such an idiot! I really thought I was doing the right thing… "

"Taking me to the beach is the right thing," she soothed.

"Yes, it'll give you a bit of peace before your sisters start fussing over your hair and dress, asking a million questions, wanting selfies and attention…"

"Exactly!"

"I didn't think of it. Austin did. When he rang to arrange it, I saw how absolutely right for you he is and that I'd have to get over my silly fantasy of us getting back together. Wishing you well for your wedding, and helping it get off to a good start seemed like the first step, so I made sure I got that booking. I just never considered how you'd react to seeing me again. I'm so sorry."

"It's OK. It was a shock, but I can see you didn't intend that."

He reached for her hand, then thought better of it. "You have your walk. I'll be here waiting for you. Waiting to take you to your mum's I mean. Then I'll leave you alone and start looking for someone I can make happy."

"There will be someone. You're a good man, just…"

"Just not right for you? Yes, I get that now. Go on. Go for your walk."

Dinah strode out briskly, taking deep breaths of cold, salty air. At first her thoughts were in turmoil, but the sea and the peace soothed her. By the time she turned to come back, she was calm again and looking forward to the joyful chaos which would greet her at Mum's.

Robert opened the car door for her, just as she reached it. "Ready?" he asked.

"Yes, I'm ready."

From this moment on she'd rarely be alone, as even when they weren't side by side, her heart and thoughts would be with Austin and his with her. The realisation she didn't want it any other way filled her with calm, peace and love.

Thank you for reading this book. I hope you enjoyed it. If you did, I'd really appreciate it if you could leave a short review on Amazon and/or Goodreads.

To learn more about my writing life, hear about new releases and get a free short story, sign up to my newsletter – https://mailchi.mp/677f65e1ee8f/sign-up or you can find the link on my website patsycollins.uk

Patsy's latest crime novel

ACTING LIKE A KILLER

Amelia Watson needs a dead body by tea time. Less urgent, but more important are – time for a life, the chance to solve crime, an uncomplicated romantic relationship, promotion at work, to be less hurt by her parents' distance. And then there's Nicole, and the attractive stranger...

Of course Amelia doesn't get all she desires, or appreciate everything that life brings. Along the way her priorities change and she ends up with far more than she'd bargained for. Will the unexpected bonus break her heart?

Chapter 1

Honestly, how could anyone be too ill to die? And where on earth was she going to find someone else willing to be bashed over the head with a blunt instrument in twelve hours' time?

"Next year will be very different," vowed Amelia Watson, duty manager of Falmouth's largest hotel. Rather than devise an interesting scheme to boost the usual pre-festive season slump in business, and avoid mid-November tinsel, she would embrace Christmas starting early. Why wait until next year? She immediately made New Year's resolutions. "I'll avoid everything to do with crime of all kinds, particularly murders and dead bodies. And if I get any more brilliant ideas I'll keep them to myself," she promised, very quietly, whilst printing an itemised receipt. It didn't count unless you wrote it down or said it out loud.

As Amelia processed the fidgeting queue of guests checking out, she allowed her attention to drift to the man waiting patiently at the back. Partly because he was pleasant to look at. Mostly to avoid thinking about the impending disaster which would begin with the far longer queue who'd soon attempt to check in.

"We hope to see you again soon," she told a departing guest, then, "How can I help you?" to the next in line.

He didn't want to be helped. He wanted a discount for not having a sea view, because gulls existed, and the fact it had rained on Wednesday. Amelia, politely but firmly, charged the price he'd been quoted for the room he'd booked. Thankfully there were just seven people left for Amelia to deal with, and the attractive man at the back wasn't a complainer. She could always tell.

Although it was great that The Fal View was fully booked, it would have been better if they were also fully staffed. Increased bookings proved Amelia's idea had been excellent. Had, past tense. A quarter of her staff getting colds was inconvenient, but not a complete shock during November. Amelia had just about cajoled enough people to take extra shifts when the real snag arose – one which was in no way her fault and which she simply couldn't have anticipated. No corpse.

Available from November 28th 2021 as a paperback and ebook.

More Books by Patsy Collins

Novels

Firestarter
Escape To The Country
A Year And A Day
Paint Me A Picture
Leave Nothing But Footprints

Non-fiction –

From Story Idea To Reader
(co-written with Rosemary J. Kind)

A Year Of Ideas:
365 sets of writing prompts and exercises

Short story collections –

Over The Garden Fence
Up The Garden Path
Through The Garden Gate
In The Garden Air

No Family Secrets
Can't Choose Your Family
Keep It In The Family
Family Feeling
Happy Families

All That Love Stuff
With Love And Kisses
Lots Of Love
Love Is The Answer

Slightly Spooky Stories I
Slightly Spooky Stories II
Slightly Spooky Stories III
Slightly Spooky Stories IV

Just A Job
Perfect Timing
A Way With Words
Dressed To Impress
Coffee & Cake
Not A Drop To Drink

Printed in Great Britain
by Amazon